FLOATING ON

The Story of Noah

FLOATING ON

FAITH

written by

David Boudreaux

TATE PUBLISHING & *Enterprises*

Published by Tate Publishing & Enterprises, LLC
127 E. Trade Center Terrace | Mustang, Oklahoma 73064 USA
1.888.361.9473 | www.tatepublishing.com

Tate Publishing is committed to excellence in the publishing industry. The company reflects the philosophy established by the founders, based on Psalm 68:11,
"The Lord gave the word and great was the company of those who published it."

Book design copyright © 2009 by Tate Publishing, LLC. All rights reserved.
Cover & interior design by Kellie Southerland
Illustrated by Kurt Jones

Published in the United States of America

ISBN: 978-1-60696-963-2
1. Juvenile Fiction: Religious: Christian: People & Places
2. Juvenile Fiction: Religious: Christian: Values & Virtues
09.06.11

DEDICATION

To my beautiful daughter, Hannah, who inspired this book, and to my lovely wife, Luci, who gave constant encouragement, feedback, and support throughout this process. God bless them.

TABLE OF CONTENTS

THE BIRTH OF NOAH

When Lamech had lived 182 years, he had a son. He named him Noah and said, "He will comfort us in the labor and painful toil of our hands caused by the ground the LORD has cursed."

Genesis 5:28–29

Lamech was troubled. It was becoming more and more dangerous to go into the village these days. It seemed that everywhere he turned, he witnessed another crime, saw more and more corruption and sin. He turned to enter his home, shutting out the world for another evening. In all his 182 years, it had been this way. It was hard to distinguish whom to trust, except his own family members. But even some of those from Adam's and Seth's sons and daughters had moved away and become a part of the wickedness that was so rampant.

He looked over at his wife; she would be giving birth at any time. She looked up at him and smiled. That was what Lamech needed in that moment. He closed his eyes, turned his face heavenward, and began to speak to God, who was reminding him of all the blessings in his life on which he should focus and be thankful!

He was blessed with a loving, faithful, obedient wife, a place to call home, and most of all, a mighty sovereign God that protected and guided him all of his days. He prayed silently, a personal prayer to God, thanking and praising him for keeping them safe despite all the evil in the world around them. He thanked God for his father and his grandfather, who walked with God even now. He praised the God that his father had raised him to worship and know—the mighty creator of the heavens, the earth, and all things in them. He felt a reassurance and peace settle over him as he finished his prayers. Lamech turned again to his wife.

She seemed more restless than usual tonight. Over the past few weeks, and more frequently tonight, he noticed her close her eyes, tighten her jaw, become tense all over her body, and then relax. Except for a visible tightening of her jaw and her body, Lamech could see no visible signs in the dim light of the pains of childbirth beginning in earnest.

There was a noise outside, and Lamech moved quickly to the entrance to see what it was. He was expecting company, but he knew he must use caution in these days. After a muffled response to his question, Lamech went out to greet his father, Methuselah, and his mother. Enoch's wife and daughters were with them. Enoch was his grandfather. He greeted each of the women with a hug and they went inside.

Lamech stayed out with his father, and they hugged one another roughly. Methuselah and Lamech walked out into the night, lit by the glow of a full moon. They spoke of the blessings associated with the miracle going on inside the house and the responsibilities associated with raising a child properly in the eyes of God. Lamech prayed silently that he could be the example that his father and his grandfather had been to him as he was growing up.

The discussion turned to the world around them. The people surrounding them seemed to be so far from God, and it was difficult for Lamech and Methuselah to understand how that could have happened. They knew that without God being a part of their lives, they would feel so empty, so lost. But they didn't dwell on those thoughts and soon turned again to discuss the birth of Lamech's first child, soon to be born.

It must have been hours later, though it didn't seem that much time had passed, when Lamech suddenly looked up from where he and his father were stooped, tracing diagrams in the dirt. He turned toward his home and listened intently. There it was again in the distance; he was certain now that he heard a baby's cry!

He jumped to his feet and smiled broadly down at his father. It was hard for him to contain himself, but he helped Methuselah rise up. His father was moving too slowly for Lamech. Though he was only 369, he was not as agile and quick as his son. He grinned at Lamech and motioned for him to go on, that he would follow behind. Lamech dashed off toward the wonderful sound in the distance. Methuselah followed as quickly as his aging body would take him. He was anxious to see his grandchild, but he knew that his wife would have him wait outside until the new family had sufficient time to say their first hellos to one another.

As he walked, he thought of family. He was now four years older than his father was when he went to walk with God. A large part of him rejoiced at the thought of his father, not taken by death, but in heaven at this very moment walking with God. But there was a part of him that missed his father terribly. Enoch had been a great father. He gave Methuselah the values that he had passed on to Lamech, and he prayed Lamech would be passing them on to his child. He began to pray to God to bless this family and all of their ways. He prayed that this child would never stray from the path God had chosen for him.

Methuselah knew that his own path had not always been as straight as he would have liked, but he knew that their God was merciful. And he was grateful that he had never strayed far before God showed him the way once again. He smiled as he realized he could no longer hear the baby's cry. Life was good.

The stillness was shattered by a high-pitched scream from the direction of the village. It was a scream that sent shivers up his spine and made the hairs stand up on his arms. Methuselah did not want to know what made the sound or what had caused it to make the sound. He shook his head. "Not tonight, God," he prayed. "Shut out the world tonight. We will deal with the world tomorrow."

As Methuselah drew near to the dwelling, he saw Lamech coming forth carrying his child. The moon was certainly bright that night, but it paled in comparison to the new father's face. Methuselah looked over at his own wife who stood patiently by, smiling. She gazed over at her husband walking toward her, nodded her head, and smiled at him, as though she were back 182 years at the time of the birth of her first child. That child was bringing his first child out to meet his grandfather. Once again Methuselah turned his thoughts, his praise, and worship to his almighty God—a God who had reasons totally unknown to Methuselah to bless a simple man in so many ways in a brief lifetime.

"Father, meet Noah!" Lamech was beaming as he held out the newborn child. The child was squirming but seemed content in his father's arms. He was obviously adjusting well to his totally new surroundings. "Noah! That is a good name for your son; 'rest,' yes, that is a good name for your boy!"

Methuselah put his hand on Lamech's shoulder. It may have been that Methuselah had gone back in time himself as his wife had and was remembering Lamech's own birth. And now here was his son, holding his grandson before him, proclaiming his name. "Thank you, Yahweh." Methuselah seemed to be beaming just a little himself.

Lamech raised his son, who was wrapped in a light blanket, toward the heavens and gave thanks to God for a healthy child and for his wife who was resting quietly inside. He paused for a moment in quiet prayer, and God gave him the blessing to proclaim for his son. "Noah, he will comfort us in the labor and painful toil of our hands caused by the ground the LORD has cursed." Lamech could feel, rather than hear, God's words come to him. God was not speaking to many families of the earth these days. But his words were given to Lamech for this new child.

Lamech's thoughts went to his family, and he felt so proud of his son, grateful for his father, mother, wife, and his life. He looked over at his father, and Methuselah's eyes caught Lamech by surprise. There was a look that spoke volumes to him, and in that moment as their eyes locked, a father passed on a generation of advice, wisdom, and love. It was an unspoken message between him and his father; it was a culmination of the lessons, values, and morals that had been kept alive for generations and passed on to Lamech. It was the understanding and knowledge that the LORD would guide Lamech as he passed these same things on to his son and then Noah to his sons. There was only peace and thankfulness in the moments of silence that followed.

As Lamech lowered his son and looked down into his little eyes, Lamech's mother proclaimed that it was time to prepare a meal. There were hungry men, who hadn't realized they were hungry, and a tired wife inside that needed nourishment and rest. They all turned to go in, and for the first time, the new father noticed the small crowd that had gathered just outside the home, watching all that had taken place. Lamech's aunts had quietly slipped out to witness the naming and the blessing of his little one. Some were wiping tears from their eyes and all were smiling as they turned back inside.

The smell of the food filled their little home, and it was then that the men realized they were famished. Lamech brought Noah over to his wife who was quietly resting. She had heard the blessing from inside, and of course, she and Lamech had long been discussing the name of their firstborn. Noah, meaning rest, seemed like a very good idea to her at the moment. She accepted her new son and her husband's kiss as he handed the child to her. And that night the Spirit of the LORD was over their home. And no sounds from without could be heard; no hint of the outside world for the remainder of that evening penetrated the thoughts of those within. All slept well into the morning. And it was a beautiful morning!

A CHANGING WORLD

The LORD saw how great man's wickedness on the earth had become, and that every inclination of the thoughts of his heart was only evil all the time. The LORD was grieved that he had made man on the earth, and his heart was filled with pain.

Genesis 6:5–6

Noah grew quickly into a fine young man, obedient to his parents and elders, always ready to help with whatever needed to be done. His father brought him up in the ways that his father had raised him and his father before that. Lamech was passing on the things that had been passed on to him: his heritage and their knowledge and faith in God. When Lamech had been only fifty-six years old, Adam, then 930 years old, had passed away, taken back to the dust from whence he came. Lamech told Noah that Adam was the first man created by God. This was hard for Noah to grasp, but his father had already spoken of faith and believing in things even if you could not see them. So Noah believed.

Just eight years before Noah had been born, Adam's son

Seth passed away. But both Adam and Seth had borne many sons and daughters. Not much was spoken of Adam's other son, Cain. Noah knew the facts about Cain and his brother Abel, but what had become of Cain was hushed rather than spoken of openly—around Noah, anyway.

Noah especially liked to hear about his great-grandfather, Enoch. He wanted to follow God as Enoch had followed him. He wasn't sure if he wanted to be "taken up" as Enoch had, but there grew in Noah a love of this God he could not see. He had an appreciation and thankfulness of this sovereign Creator for all he had done for past generations and for his immediate family.

Noah used to watch intently as his mother and father prayed together. They began each day in prayer; they prayed before each meal and ended each day the same way—giving thanks and praise to God. His father had told him that throughout the day he would often think of God and pause to praise and glorify his name. And it was not done out of an obligation or supposed duty, but of a love and desire to know and be nearer to him. And Noah was growing up the same way. At an early age, he began to pray beside his parents whenever he could. He tried to remember, as he busied himself throughout the day, to pause and remember to give thanks to God as his father had taught him.

Lamech also taught Noah to use caution and great care around others. He tried to explain the nature of people in the surrounding areas and the areas of their extended family. The stories and recounts seemed to be the same wherever the news came from. People were more interested in their own welfare, their own greedy nature, and their own sinful desires.

They had no desire to follow God or give him thanks and praise. Accounts of rampant theft, cheating, lies, murder, and immorality seemed to be evident everywhere. Lamech tried to teach Noah how to be cautious and use common sense in those times he had to be around strangers. He told him also to use wise judgment around some of his own aunts and uncles. Lamech did not want Noah to become a hermit or recluse but to be aware that men would try to convince him to join in their evil plans and schemes and to seek false gods.

Enosh, the son of Seth, passed away at 905 years of age. At only eighty-four, death was very unfamiliar to Noah. He had heard stories of people being killed, but that only happened to the wicked that served idols and would have nothing to do with God. He did not understand how these people could have gotten so far from God. If he tried to speak of God to them, they dismissed his ideas as being farfetched, even crazy! Some were mean to him, and others just got away from him as quickly as they could.

Noah knew the wonderful feeling of God's presence, and he could not identify with those people who had no desire to be near to him. But he found he had little success in his endeavors to convince people of their foolish ways. Even those that seemed to receive his message about his loving God did not express any interest in changing or following after God themselves; it did not seem to take root. Typically, if he saw them again, they were living the same way they had been before he spoke with them. He noticed that even childhood acquaintances were being swallowed up in the world and its increasingly wicked ways.

When he was still a young man of only two hundred years, Noah ventured out on his own. He did not leave his family because he was unhappy or due to any conflict, but he felt a calling to be among those of the world. He could not explain it to his father, but he felt a need to speak to more people about the God he served and worshipped. He knew there was a danger of becoming like those in the world, accepting gods of every shape, form, and temperament one could dream up. But his faith in the one true God, the God that never changed, who was the same as he had always been, was strong. And he felt the very Spirit of God with him.

Lamech gave Noah his blessings the day Noah left. There were assurances to one another that they would see each other again, that Noah would let his family know he was well, and that God was protecting him. When he started out, he was full of anticipation of the things God had in store for him. One prayer of Noah's that he had not shared with his family was the desire to find a wife. Many women had expressed interest in the young man, but Noah did not feel that any of them were the one woman he was waiting for. More often than not, they came along with a bounty of gods they were more than eager to share with whoever their new husband would be. And Noah would not tolerate that. His father had been very understanding, even considering his age. No one in his family had ever reached two hundred years without children, much less a wife. But Noah knew the LORD had someone special in mind for him. She just did not seem to be in the territory where his family lived.

So, Noah traveled the countryside visiting villages and towns mingling with the citizens and sharing his faith with them. Some were very receptive to the message. Unfortunately, it typically turned out that they were more than happy to add another "god" to their inventory. Others were opposed to the idea that Noah's God was any better than those they had already established to worship. Reactions from these types ranged from verbal indignation to violent opposition. Depending on the crowds, Noah found himself making hasty retreats on more than one occasion. He could not call his ministry fruitful by any means, but for nearly one hundred years, Noah faithfully traveled the lands seeking those of similar faith or those who would be interested in knowing about his faith.

True to his word, Noah kept in touch with his family, visiting now and then. His father and grandfather confirmed the seeming decline in morals around them that Noah saw everywhere he went. Together they wondered how long it could possibly go on. They knew God would not tolerate this forever.

Finally Noah decided to settle down and build himself a home. He was not forsaking the calling he felt to reach out to his fellow man. He was simply putting down roots and establishing a place he could return to from time to time. He chose a region of rolling hills and fertile valleys as his homestead. He built a small home up on one large, wide ridge overlooking a beautiful valley in the direction of the rising sun. Over time, he planted crops and a vineyard and began raising livestock. He ventured out less frequently, experiencing a sense of peace as he cultivated the land and cared for his home.

He had not given up on his desire to find a good woman to share his life with, but he had been discouraged by what he had seen in his travels. There was a village about a day's journey to the east from where he had settled, and Noah periodically made his way there to trade and visit and to see if any of the people were ripe for God's blessings; it was usually a disappointing trip. In previous visits he also noticed there were particular areas of the village that seemed darker than others. When he entered from the west, that area was growing in population and depravity. It used to be subtle, but with each visit, usually only once a year, it had spread. He could sense the evil and wickedness the moment he entered the village. He would just quicken his pace to the center of the village and the marketplace where he would conduct his business and mingle with the citizens and visitors.

On one particular visit, he was bartering for some fresh fruit he had not seen in this area for years. It looked very appealing to him. But the man offering the produce was a shrewd businessman who was very experienced at bargaining. Noah was no easy prey, and soon the negotiations became quite animated and yet remained civil.

"A basket of my grapes for a basket of your fruit is more than fair." Noah waved his arms at each of the items as his voice grew louder. "My baskets are much larger than yours. So you are actually receiving the greater gain."

The man shook his head even before Noah finished. "You cannot find this fruit anywhere near this region. Not this type, and definitely not of this quality." The man picked up a sample and shook it at Noah. *This is getting good!* the trader thought. This man before him was no pushover, and he liked that. This was a good negotiation to start his day. And the man continued. "Two baskets of grapes for a basket of my delicacy is a fair bargain, I would say!" He motioned to the donkey behind Noah, which was laden with freshly harvested grapes.

Noah quickly realized his disadvantage by the man being able to see how much he had to offer. The man had wisely displayed only a small portion of what he had. Noah decided to test his theory that there was much more hidden in the tent just behind the trader. "If I consider such a preposterous offer, how many baskets of 'your delicacies' might I get?" Noah acted indignant by the offer, but the fruit certainly looked inviting.

"Metis!" The vendor yelled into the tent behind his display. "Bring out more of our gifts from the gods!" His mouth curved up into a smile as he spoke. Noah tensed at the reference to "gift of the gods." But he had become so used to hearing that same spiel he hid his reaction and smiled back at the man.

The flap of the tent waved open, and out stepped a young woman carrying two baskets of fruit. Her face was covered by a cloth veil. Only her eyes were visible. Noah looked at her, and his heart seemed to skip a beat! The beautiful dark eyes of the man's daughter met his as she straightened up. She too seemed surprised as she hesitated, though only briefly. She carried the baskets over to her father. He looked at his daughter suspiciously as she handed him the fruit.

"How much are you interested in?" the man asked, determined to get back to business. He motioned for his daughter to go back to the tent. She lowered her eyes and head and made her way back toward the entrance of the tent. "I don't know when or if I will ever be back this way again. This may be your last chance to sample my wares." He wanted to close in and seal the deal with this man quickly. But Noah was completely captivated by the beauty about to disappear into the tent.

"Wait!" Noah shouted toward the daughter. Instantly realizing this was inappropriate behavior, he diverted his eyes to her father. But it was too late. The man had seen where Noah's attention had been. Metis also noticed, and this man's boldness surprised her so much she stopped in her tracks and stared at the stranger before her. As his eyes had turned away, she found herself staring at him. "I mean," Noah fumbled with his thoughts, "is this all that you have?" He waved his hand over the display before him.

When the father's eyes followed Noah's hand to the fruit, Noah seized the opportunity to look back at the woman at the opening of the tent. His eyes caught hers before she could look away. She blushed as she realized how brazen she was being. And now she had been caught at it! She was drawn to this stranger, though she did not know why. She was embarrassed by the situation. Noah too realized he had been overly bold and was ashamed by the obvious discomfort he was causing this lovely woman.

Again her father caught Noah's eyes as they turned from the direction of his daughter. He turned to face her and saw the red blush. It was obvious even behind the veil. Suddenly the man's mind, shrewd businessman above all else, realized he had an opportunity here. He had been trying to get rid of his daughter for years! She was a burden to him, and all attempts to marry her off had been unsuccessful. She was opinionated and too wise for her own good.

Metis hurried into the tent. As soon as the flap had closed behind her, she let out a frustrated gasp of air and threw up her arms. She was surprised at her shameless behavior! This man had a quality about him that had drawn her to him. But if he was the man of integrity she thought he might be, he would surely have been repelled by her actions. She clenched her jaw together, but then it started to soften. She thought of how their eyes had met again. She slumped down, not sure what to think or do.

"I see your mind is not on fruit any longer. Perhaps our business is done here." The man decided to gamble on what he thought might be multiple opportunities here. "Please take your things and move on. You are hindering others that may be truly interested in my goods." He looked beyond Noah into the crowded marketplace. But he kept him in his peripheral view, looking for signs of weakness. They were there!

Noah panicked, though he was not sure why. He tried to keep his composure. "What are you referring to? I have grapes and you have fruit. If you are not interested in my grapes, the best there are anywhere around here by the way, please tell me now." Noah wanted to keep up the dialogue, but he knew he could not put himself in the position this man was trying get him in, one of desperation. As he waited for a response, he prayed a silent prayer to God. "Lord, give me the right words to say. Soften this man's hard heart. Let me speak with this woman, if it be your will."

Once again, the man was impressed. He knew he had the upper hand, but he would have to play this out to the end. He liked the challenge. He reminded himself not to get too anxious about the thought of unloading his daughter. "You seemed otherwise occupied." The man narrowed his eyes as he turned to Noah. "As you will not be my only visitor today, I think we should conclude our business quickly." He motioned back toward the tent. "Your stares and ogling at my precious daughter are not welcome. You are not subtle in your advances, and I assure you they are not welcome!" He raised his voice some, but not high enough to draw the attention of the crowd around.

Inside the tent, Metis heard her father carrying on. *Oh, come now!* she thought. She heaved another sigh. *My precious daughter, my foot!* Her father had often told her of his frustrated efforts to unload her. She listened closely as the stranger held his own against her father. She was impressed. Did she dare hope? Did she dare have faith? Despite her father's willingness to take on any gods that might help him make a sale, there was no evidence that she had faith in any of them.

She could not hear the entire conversation because of the other sounds from the marketplace, but she could tell that the stranger and her father were still talking. After some time, it got quiet. She feared her father might have scared off this man she was drawn to. Something in her conscience told her not to be afraid of this man, to have faith. She edged closer to the entrance of the tent, beside the stacks of fruit. She leaned forward trying to hear what, if anything, was going on. Suddenly the tent flap flew open, and her father poked his head in looking for her. She was startled but quickly composed herself. By the time he noticed her, she was pretending to be organizing the fruit in the baskets.

He sneered at her and motioned for her to come out. She looked at him bewildered as he impatiently made a jerking motion for her to come quickly. She was nervous as she rose, but a peace came upon her like an unheard assurance of a loving father. It was nothing like the father she knew. She rose and followed him out. As she straightened up, her heart leapt when she saw the stranger still there. There were several baskets of grapes on the ground, and the man was securing baskets of their fruit to his animal.

He finished quickly and turned back to the tent. He smiled as he noticed her standing there. "This man is interested in speaking with you." Her father's tone was one of near contempt. "I have told him he could wed you, but he seems interested in what *you* might think of that." He rolled his eyes. What was this world coming to? A man asking what a woman thought! This stranger was just asking for trouble.

The daughter looked surprised at Noah. She did not understand, but she was glad at the same time. Marriages were usually arranged without any input from the woman. She knew she had been a thorn in her father's side after she had run off more than one prospect her father had come up with. She just knew in her heart she was not supposed to be with those men. When she had tried to explain to her father, he was not interested in her reasons. When she was a young girl, he would beat her. But he had not laid a hand on her for some time. She smiled thinking about the last time he had tried that. She didn't know what had come over her, but it had been the last time he ever tried!

Noah saw the hint of a smile as the corner of her eyes wrinkled slightly. He was stricken with this woman. But he wanted no part of a marriage that God did not bless. If the woman did not want to be with him, she did not belong with him, regardless of what a father might decide for his daughter. He reached his hand out to hers.

"If you will," he looked directly into her beautiful dark eyes, "I would like you to walk with me. I would like to talk with you." In spite of his calm tone, his stomach was in knots, and he felt like his heart was skipping every other beat, as if he were a young lad! He sensed that God was telling him this was the woman he had been waiting for over three hundred years. If she said no, however, he did not know what he would do.

Her eyes got larger and looked even lovelier to Noah. Her heart began to race as she realized she was reaching her hand out to his. As their hands met and he gently pulled her closer, she lowered her eyes, not looking into his any longer. *Oh great!* she thought, *I've found someone that I'm attracted to and now I'm gong to become proper and start acting aloof?* She wanted to share with him the sense she had about him, but she couldn't. It was not appropriate. But Noah thought she was perfect—for him.

Her father watched the momentary exchange. Then he watched as they turned and walked into the crowd, each one glancing now and then at one another. Both were blushing like awkward children. He realized that he had a serious opportunity to have his daughter finally married off.

Noah and Metis lost track of time as they wandered through the marketplace. Noah had practically no idea where they were going, but somehow they stayed clear of those parts of the village that no decent person should ever go. Noah talked about where he had come from and what his life was like. Metis thought it was wonderful. And she shared with him her thoughts and her dreams. Noah felt as though he had known her for a lifetime. She was very smart but not pretentious. And she was beautiful! She had taken her veil down, and Noah was convinced there was no creation of God more beautiful than the woman at his side.

It was several hours later before they noticed they were back at the place they had started. Her father was busy with a customer, but when he saw them coming, he quickly finished his business and sent the customer on his way. Both Noah and Metis were still smiling. They were making eyes at one another too. Something deep inside the man reminded him of a time that he felt like that. But he quickly blew it off as a fantasy. He needed to get his man in and seal the deal. He was determined not to have to leave this village with Metis in tow.

Lamech and his sons were coming in from the fields after a long day. Just ahead, he could see his wife around the fire outside their home cooking their supper. He could see his other children around, but there seemed to be new faces among them. As he drew closer, he realized he recognized one of the faces. It was Noah! He quickened his pace as he called to his sons behind him, "Come quick, Noah has come home!" He always loved when Noah found time to visit the family. He had long ceased trying to convince him to come back home to stay. He knew that God had called Noah to do just as he was doing.

Noah was talking with his mother and sisters as the evening meal was roasting over the open fire. He stood with his arm around Metis introducing his bride-to-be. His mother immediately ran over and embraced Metis. It surprised the young woman to be welcomed so readily and so completely. She looked over at Noah as the mother and sisters took turns embracing her, some, like his mother, more than once. Noah's mother turned and embraced him, whispering in his ear as she hugged him tightly, "I knew God would lead you to the right woman for you." She kissed his cheek and stepped away, smiling broadly at her son.

It was then she saw Lamech and her sons running up the path. Noah turned in the direction she was looking just in time to see the bulk of his father grab him in a bear hug. Metis laughed as both men stumbled backwards nearly falling over. "Noah!" his father bellowed, "it is so good to see you again. What a wonderful blessing God has given us this day!"

His brothers came up taking turns shaking his arm and hugging their brother they had not seen in years. When the initial greetings were over, Noah stepped over his father and took him by the shoulders. "Father, I know you have given up all hope long ago." He began turning his father around, as Lamech looked puzzled by the comment. "But," Noah continued, "there is someone I would like you to meet." Noah turned his father to face Metis, standing in the midst of his daughters. Lamech had not noticed the additional face among the other women. His attention had been on his son.

Noah let go of his father and took a step to Metis and reached his hand out to her. She was still smiling so broadly at the greeting between the men her cheeks were beginning to hurt. She reached her hand to Noah and stepped to his side. Lamech's eyes grew wide and his smile became broader as he realized this woman had come with his son. "Father, I would like you to meet Metis. She has agreed to be my wife." Noah had not finished his announcement, and his father was hugging her and kissing her on the cheeks.

She was taken aback when the man had showed as much, perhaps more, acceptance than the women. This was not something she was accustomed to at all. Lamech turned to Noah when he finally let her go and again embraced his son with another great bear hug. "Hah! This is wonderful! When were you married? Do we have any young Noahs on the way yet?" He laughed.

"Father, we wanted your blessing before we wed. We have come here to be with you when we marry." Noah put his arm around his bride and pulled her close.

"This just keeps getting better!" Lamech laughed. "Everyone!" He turned to the family. "We have to prepare for a wedding!" Cheers and shouts went up from the family and friends that had gathered from the community. "Come! We have much to do!" But Noah's mother stepped in front of her husband who was about to start giving orders.

"I think," she told him sternly, "we can take time for our dinner." She smiled at her husband's excitement. "The wedding plans can start in the morning. Let's have some food and visit tonight. I'm sure Noah and Metis are weary from their long journey." She rescued Metis from Lamech and led her to a place to sit where they could talk as she finished the meal preparations with her daughters.

There was much talking, laughing, and merry-making well into the night after the meal was finished. Metis felt as though she had found a home she had never known but only dreamed of.

Early the next morning, Lamech sent one of his sons out to surrounding family and friends to tell them of the wedding. People came from all around over the next few days for the wedding celebration. It lasted more than a week, and even then, some thought it had ended too soon. There had been an abundance of food and drink. There had been an abundance of laughing, music, and dancing. And among Lamech, Methuselah, Noah, and few others, there was abundance of prayer, worship, and thanks to God.

Others that felt a need to worship their multiple gods either restrained while they were at the wedding or left to return later. It was known that no worship to anyone but the one true God was allowed at this home. Metis watched all this with great interest. It told her volumes about the man she had married and his immediate family. The faith of these few was especially evident among such a large a crowd of wedding guests. She had a lot to learn about this God and faith. But she felt at peace and very safe with these people.

Finally the time came for Noah and his wife to leave. He too had a home, fields, and livestock to look after. They were sad to go, and all were sad to see them leave. There were promises between the newlyweds and their family to visit each other when possible. Then prayers for a safe journey, long life, and blessed days were shared before their journey home began.

Years passed and Noah continued to walk with God. Metis was another of the multitude of blessings that God had seen fit to give him. He could not understand how or why the LORD expressed so much favor. He was convinced that it had absolutely nothing to do with him and everything to do with God. Over and over he would pray to understand more fully what God's will was—not only for himself, but for his family, for all his relatives, and at times, for all the people in the land.

The woman God chose for him had quickly become his best friend, his confidant, and his partner. His father, grandfather, and most other relatives now lived far away. It took days to reach their homes, and the visits became less frequent as the years passed. But whenever he felt the need to visit, his wife didn't complain. In fact, it seemed she always smiled. And often in the darkest of times, that smile could light up the room. She seemed as eager to visit his family as he did.

Noah knew that the bond between his mother and his wife had grown strong over the years. Perhaps it was because of the family from which she had come. She wouldn't speak much of them, and Noah didn't push. But he felt as though there was a deep sorrow and perhaps some fear associated with those memories. And the last thing he ever wanted to do was to stir up any fear or hurt in this beautiful woman that had agreed to spend her life with him.

Whenever Noah grew despondent, Metis would try her best to cheer him. The worst times were when he felt he had been a disappointment to God, like when he compared his walk with God to his father's walk, or his lack of patience with the pagans and their multitudes of gods, or even just the way he became distracted from prayer on some days. She would quickly remind him of the God he had told her about, the same one his father had told him about. He had shared that their God would be a forgiving, loving, gracious God and not at all like the gods that were being worshipped by those around them.

As he thought about their false worship, it was only with the greatest of restraints that he didn't pound these pagans into the dust. God had done so much for him, and he found it very difficult to tolerate these idol worshipers he encountered.

One day as Noah busied himself working the earth, he felt a strong urge that he should be doing something different. He paused and straightened up from his work, wiping his brow with his forearm, trying to focus on this feeling that seemed to come upon him so strongly. He struggled as he reasoned in his mind that he had plenty to do right where he was. As he wondered about all this, he looked back over the grapevines, particularly the area he had begun working in this morning.

Noah was a man of the soil, and the LORD had seen fit to bless him with a green thumb.

In addition to his vineyard, which was not so small, he also grew a variety of herbs and vegetables. He cultivated the ground himself and irrigated the crops by hand and occasionally drew water from a nearby water source. But most of the time the dew that God sent up from the ground was sufficient to keep his gardens thriving.

He had a modest herd of sheep, goats, and a pair of fine oxen that he was able to graze near his home. Even in the changing seasons, he did not have to venture far from his home to find suitable feedstock for his animals. And at times he would trade in the village for those things he did not raise himself. But for the most part, the LORD had allowed Noah and his wife to be self-sufficient. Noah smiled as he thought of how blessed this little household most certainly was.

But the gnawing feeling that he should be doing something else would not leave him, regardless of how much he tried to focus. He looked again over this land that the LORD had given him stewardship. Then he looked at the fruits of his labor. He tried to go back to working the vines, but eventually he gave in to the calling and turned toward home. Perhaps his wife needed him for something. But as he turned to go, something told him that this was not the answer.

When he arrived home, he found his wife busy with her own daily duties. She was pleasantly surprised to see her husband home so early. She greeted him with a hug and a big smile, and for a brief moment, Noah forgot why he had left the fields in the first place. When she asked him why he was home so early, he felt a slight twinge of guilt as he explained it was not because he missed her or that he had just wanted to surprise her. Of course there was no reason for him to feel guilty, and as he explained his feeling and his thought that she may need him for something, she noticed the seriousness in his voice and in his eyes. There was something bothering her husband and distracting him from his work.

As he explained the sense he had that he should be doing

something else, she earnestly tried to help him figure what that could be. After a few suggestions, none of which seemed right to Noah, his wife took his hands and looked deep into his eyes. She suggested that they move to a shaded place nearby and pray for God to reveal what Noah should do. Perhaps they could discern from the LORD if this was from him or not.

They prayed that the LORD would speak clearly to Noah. They praised and worshipped his name and gave him thanks for the multitude of blessings he gave them each day. Metis got up after several moments, but he stayed to pray longer. She kissed his forehead and went back to her chores but continued to silently pray for her husband to receive guidance.

She looked back over her shoulder at him as he prayed on his knees with his eyes closed and his face turned toward the heavens. She felt certain that he would get his answer. Not because he deserved it, but because of her husband's connection and his relationship with the Creator of all things. God seemed to have his hand on her husband's life.

Just moments later, Noah came in and explained to his wife that he would be going into the village this day. She asked half jokingly if he had given up trying to figure why he was so restless. It went completely over his head, and he seemed to be in a hurry to get started. When she asked if he knew what he was to do, he told his wife he had no idea but knew this was where he should go. He held her very close for a long while. It was always a wonderful feeling to hold her close to his chest.

He insisted on leaving right away, but there was no way his wife would let him leave without taking some food and drink. It was not a long journey, but she figured if he didn't know what he was going for, he couldn't possibly know when he would return. And even if he returned today, it would be very late before he made it all the way home. She would not have her husband going hungry or thirsty!

As he started out, Noah looked back at his wife who was standing and watching him. And while he was reminding himself to praise God for such a fine woman, she was praising God and praying her own prayers. She was asking God to keep her husband safe and bring him back quickly. She prayed that God would reveal his plan clearly to her husband and give him the skills, strength, wisdom, discernment, whatever he would need to carry out God's will this day.

As Noah was drawing near the village, he decided he should enter the community from the east, rather than the south. It would have certainly been much closer to go in from the south, but it had seemed to Noah that when he ventured this way, he always encountered people of questionable character. There seemed to be more fights and brawls, more theft and all sorts of goings-on that he preferred to avoid altogether. So he decided to make a wide circle to his left, well outside the parameter of the settlement, and enter from the east. It puzzled Noah as to why the residents had done nothing to rid the village of this wickedness.

He still was not sure why he was here in the village. But he felt very strongly that this was just where he should be. As he made his way down the narrow passages between the mud buildings, he would come into openings like a small square or market area. Tents or makeshift shelters had been set up in front of buildings and in corners throughout the marketplace.

The number of people he saw on the east side shocked him, and as he watched them, he was perplexed. He was concerned that he may have been concentrating so much on why he was supposed to be here that he had in fact entered from the south side. People were pushing and shoving, yelling and cursing, stealing and running away in every direction he turned.

He checked out the position of the sun, looked back out at distant familiar landmarks, and determined that he had indeed come in from the east. Noah had come to know this whole region very well over the past 480 years. He was in the right place all right! But this part of the village had turned out to be just as corrupt as the areas he had hoped to avoid. He wondered if the whole settlement had declined to this level and shook his head sadly.

His heart sank, but he instinctively raised his guard. He had no business daydreaming and not paying attention to his surroundings in a place like this! That could easily lead to disaster. He kept moving into the chaos, trusting the LORD would keep him safe. He was in shock at the scene before him. He thought about how things had changed so drastically in such a short time! He moved on, trying to avoid the people moving all around, pushing and shoving to get where they thought they needed to be.

Suddenly, Noah was hit from behind and nearly knocked off his feet by a large bearded man shoving past him, half dragging a woman with him. The man had to be at least eight cubits tall (over twelve feet!). The woman he dragged along had dark hair and strangely painted eyes, lips, and face. The colors were too bright to be natural, and she did not even look real to him. She was laughing and cursing at anyone who got in the way. Though he was pulling her along, supporting her under her right arm, it was obvious she was not trying to get away from the giant. She was more like a hideous idol spitting out curses and obnoxious verses as she passed. Both were staggering as they quickly moved through the open area toward the far side, leaving behind an almost visible trail of the stench of cheap wine.

Noah figured he must be one of the Nephilim or at least one of their offspring. He had heard stories of them for a long time, but this was his first encounter with one. They were not known to inhabit these parts until recently. The stories of these giants had been told by passing travelers. Tall tales of their alleged deeds of valor and courage had made them objects of admiration to most people. Noah had heard some of these stories, and neither valor, courage, nor righteousness came to his mind as a way to describe these men. It was a discouraging sign for him that so many people held ungodly men like this in high esteem.

There was never any praise to God for the deeds of these men, but if one listened closely to the accounts of their deeds, he didn't think the LORD would want to be associated with them. Even apart from the tales that seemed to be more and more embellished each time they were repeated, the behavior of the Nephilim revealed their true nature. They did not present themselves as examples of anything Noah would want to follow. He feared that the world's idea of what defined a man of valor was very different from how God might define these Nephilim, or "fallen ones" as their name implied.

Noah did not ponder on the Nephilim for very long. There were so many people going in so many directions he had to focus fully on his surroundings or risk being knocked down and trampled. The people in the crowd around him appeared rude and hateful to one another. It was truly a sight that filled him with sorrow. Noah began to wonder why God would lead him here of all places, and he prayed that he would be delivered from the evil around him.

Just as Noah turned a corner, two young men came barreling straight toward him! It happened so fast that he had no time to move out of the way and they crashed right into him, which sent all three of them to the ground. While struggling to untangle himself from these two strangers, Noah suddenly realized the men were using this "accident" as an opportunity to steal the satchel he was carrying. Noah chastised himself for not realizing what was happening sooner or reacting faster. Still on the ground, he tried to grab at the satchel that was disappearing into the crowd.

With the bodies off him, Noah was able to rise to his feet and saw the men running with his bag. They were laughing as they ran away from him. But the density of the crowd made it impossible for him to give successful chase, so he watched the meal his wife had prepared for him that morning escape into the crowd.

Just before the thieves were about to turn down an alleyway, they stopped to rummage through the satchel. Noah peered into the crowd until he spotted them. He wasn't sure what they expected to find, but it was obviously not food and water. For each time they pulled an article out of the satchel, they tossed it to the ground, reaching in further for some elusive treasure.

For a split second, Noah thought he could reach them through the crowd since they had stopped, but he was distracted by another commotion behind him. It was coming from beyond the corner he was turning when he ran into the two thieves. He was reluctant to look closer, but he was drawn to the confusion. He could see a crowd circled around some hidden activity that was causing lots of cheering and laughing. Some seemed to be watching with joy, some with anger, and some with horror. But they stayed behind an unseen, but clearly established, line that no one could pass.

Against his better judgment but feeling as though he was being drawn in, he began to make his way into the crowd. He was knocked around as he entered in, moving toward the center of activity. Just as he was being drawn closer and closer to the point of commotion, the crowd could not appear to hold him back; each person moved aside to allow him access and closed in again behind him as he moved in. The parting crowd was not being polite in the slightest, but it was more like an unconscious parting of bodies. And never once did any of them lose their focus on the activity still unknown to Noah.

When he finally broke through to the clearing in the center of the large crowd, Noah caught sight of what had everyone's attention. As the realization of what he was seeing began to sink in, Noah could feel his temper begin to rise. Three men were beating on another man. One man held the victim from behind while a giant (Nephilim) was systematically throwing punches into the man's face, abdomen, and chest. The third man, who was of normal stature, was standing to the side of the victim, throwing punches as well as kicks to his leg and knee. He got in his blows at such times as he felt he could land them without putting himself in the way of the giant's forceful punches.

Like a peal of thunder, Noah shouted at the three, "Stop this now!" His voice was so abrupt and so loud that the entire crowd grew completely silent and the attackers ceased their blows in midswing. Everyone looked dazed for a moment.

Noah had begun to move forward the moment he had spoken, heading directly for the injured man who was barely conscious. When he reached the man, he reflexively threw out both his arms, knocking the Nephilim backwards into the crowd in one direction, as well as the man holding the victim from behind in the opposite direction. The third man stood with his mouth open; he was stunned. It looked to him like another Nephilim had attacked his companions and was making a bee-line for him! He dropped to his knees and covered his eyes, praying to some god he had heard about at some point in his miserable existence.

The beaten man never had the chance to slump to the ground. For as soon as Noah had struck the other two assailants, sending them reeling backwards, he grabbed the semiconscious man and held him up. He put the man's right arm around his shoulders and neck and supported his weight. The Nephilim was regaining his balance and, being a "man of valor," started back to attack Noah from behind. Noah did not realize he was coming, but something told him to swing around in that direction, which he did, still supporting the badly beaten victim.

His face may have still been red with anger, or perhaps the giant was drunk with wine, but the big man thought he was facing someone much larger, stronger, and fiercer than himself. He paused in his advance and just stood with his mouth open. The man before him seemed to grow larger by the second. Noah just glared back into the eyes of the giant, wanting to give him some of what he had given, but not willing to release the hold on the man he had just saved from … well, the LORD only knows.

At the very thought of the LORD's name, Noah began to calm down. He was again disheartened that this could happen in plain sight and so many could just stand by. Not one of them raised a hand to stop this brutal assault! To the Nephilim and the other men, Noah appeared to be as angry and as large and fierce as ever. Slowly the attackers backed away, turned, and disappeared into the crowd. In the meantime, the crowd had been frozen in mid-gasp. They were not sure what they had just witnessed, and most felt they could potentially be the next target of this fearless man before them.

Noah looked around at the startled faces before him. He had no idea what was going through their minds at that moment. "How could you stand by and watch this?" he began. His voice was clear and firm. "What kind of people are you that you can allow this to go on, that you can cheer it on, that you will not step in to help or at the least run away in horror? I fear the LORD is saddened deeply this day to see his children like this. I pray sincerely that he will shake each one of you to your senses. Drop now before our Creator and ask his forgiveness! Pray for his guidance in your lives from this day forth!" Noah's voice rose as he ended the sentence. Then he dropped to his knees with the injured man still supported on his shoulder so that both were kneeling. He closed his eyes and began praying for God's mercy for himself, for the injured man, for the crowd, and for the attackers. He asked forgiveness for the wickedness of the earth and for the evil in all men's hearts. He prayed the LORD would make him strong in his walk and that he would help these people to see the error of their wicked ways.

When he had finished praying, he felt revived and totally at peace. He knew he must care for the injured man, so he opened his eyes and rose up. The crowd had disappeared. There was a wide, clear space all around him, but just beyond, the market-place was carrying on as though nothing out of the ordinary had occurred.

Noah sighed deeply. He then turned away to find a place to clean this man's wounds and find him a place to rest and recover. He carried him through the streets once again, not sure where he was going. He recalled an inn that might have space where this man could recuperate. But things had changed so drastically since his last visit he was not sure where it was located. So he just continued on, assisting the man to walk as best he could.

A short time later, Noah stopped to rest while the man tried to clear his head; he was in obvious pain. They sat there for a while with their backs against the mud walls. Noah wanted to understand why this man had been selected to receive the beating he had gotten. But it was difficult for him to talk, and his breathing was labored. Noah helped him to his feet and they moved on. Just as they began moving again, a woman peered from around a corner and called for them to follow her. Noah paused, not sure whether this was safe, but the woman persisted and reluctantly he began to follow her.

She looked like one of the women from the marketplace, but not as crude as the woman he had seen with the giant earlier in the day. She brought them to a small room nearby that had a mat in one corner and a few humble furnishings placed throughout. The room was clean enough, and Noah was grateful for a place that this stranger could rest and have his wounds tended to. When he had laid him down, he began to pray that the injuries he had suffered were not as bad as they appeared.

The woman brought over a bowl of water and a piece of cloth that she used to clean away the caked blood and examine the wounds. None of them were life threatening, and as the woman cleaned him up, Noah realized he was a lucky man indeed. He would surely be sore for days to come, but he should be able to move around in a day or two.

Noah thanked the woman for her kindness to them both. This embarrassed her, and she quickly looked away to hide the smile and blush she felt rising over her face. Noah smiled back and slowly dropped to his knees to thank God for this unexpected happening. This woman, who did not have to help but chose to, was truly a gift of mercy sent by his Creator. He continued praying about all the shocking events he had seen and experienced this day. He prayed for the injured man, for the woman, and for all the people of this village. He prayed earnestly that they would seek the one true God, turn from their wicked ways, and abandon the idols of wood or stone because he knew they had no power, no mercy, and no value at all.

After a long while he stood again. And only then did he realize the woman and the beaten man had been watching him with their eyes wide and their mouths open. Something about his prayers had caught their attention. Noah thought that if he took the opportunity to reach out to them the LORD might open their hearts and minds to draw closer to him and away from the pagan gods and idols of this village.

He grinned broadly as he moved closer to them and asked if they knew the one true God. They looked at him blankly, then at one another, then back to Noah. He sat beside them and began to speak as the woman treated the man. They seemed to be listening intently to all Noah had to say. There were questions about Noah's God; there were also comparisons to the multitude of other gods these two had heard of. Noah remained patient, feeling as though the Lord was giving him the words and the power to share his truth. And this continued long after the sun had set.

When they stopped the discussion to share a small meal, Noah realized how sleepy he was. The beaten man seemed to be gaining strength by the hour and had already dozed off. Noah leaned back against the wall, rested his head on his arms over his knees, and soon nodded off as well. He slept for a few hours, and when he woke, he decided he should go home to his wife. He woke the woman and thanked her for her hospitality and kindness. He urged her to leave this place and return to her family. He told her this place was no longer for good people and urged her to escape the evil force that enveloped this village. It was dark inside and hard to read her eyes, but he was discouraged by her lack of response.

Noah stepped out into the street and looked around to get his bearings. He moved quickly and quietly through the streets until he had reached the outer edge of the village and then turned south. He was very thankful to be out of that place! There was hardly any moonlight, so he had to adjust his eyes to the night. But he really had no problem finding his way. It would likely be morning by the time he arrived home.

The nagging feelings that led him to the village had not come over him since he had found the man being attacked. He prayed as he walked, remembering the throngs of humanity. And he prayed that somehow each one of them might see the error of their ways and turn from their false gods, that they would turn from their selfish, evil, and wicked ways. Noah could not comprehend how any of them could possibly be happy living the way they were. *All they need is time*, he thought.

Then the LORD said, "My Spirit will not contend with man forever, for he is mortal; his days will be a hundred and twenty years."

Genesis 6:3

LET'S TALK

"Noah!" Noah looked up from his work and slowly turned around, expecting to see someone there with him. He was certain he had heard a voice. He wondered to himself if he really had or if he had imagined it. As clear as the voice had been, the resonance was nothing like he had ever heard. The hairs on his arms were standing up, and he had goose bumps from his wrists to his shoulders. He knew this sensation had nothing to do with the temperature on this beautiful warm and cloudless morning. He had already been working for hours though the dew, God's life-giving water for his crops, was still heavy on the leaves.

He was going to turn back to his work, but again he stopped and slowly looked around to the left and then to the right. The urge came over him to respond to the voice. Though there was no one to answer to, he could not shake the feeling that he had been called. Something came over him like a warm feeling, and he turned his face upwards to the blue sky. "My LORD?" He wanted to sound more reverent and more certain of himself, but Noah was feeling very overwhelmed. This feeling had seemed to creep up on him, and now he felt a burden, but a glorious burden, upon his shoulders. He slowly sank to his knees. "My LORD," he whispered.

"Noah, I have found you righteous and blameless among men." The voice was clearly audible to him. It was the sound of a man's voice, but at the same time, this man sounded different than any man he had ever heard speak. He continued to sink lower to the ground, and as the words from above sank in, Noah began to weep.

Again there was a confusion of emotions. Noah was weeping from an overwhelming joy that his God would speak to him. And then, beyond all comprehension, the LORD had declared him righteous and blameless among men. And thus the confusion, for Noah knew that he was not such a man. He didn't believe that God should recognize him in such a way. In his heart, Noah knew all too well that he struggled daily with unrighteous distractions in his life. He knew all the things that drew his attention from the Creator of the heavens and earth and all things therein.

Tears streamed from his eyes, and they dropped to the ground beneath his slumped body. Noah remained on his knees as he was bowed low to the point he was nearly prostrate. If he had any ability to move, he would have lain himself flat out on the ground. But he had simply sunk into this mound of flesh without any control over what he was doing.

He thought that God must have erred coming to this poor man of the earth. He was not like his great-grandfather, Enoch. Nor was he like his grandfather, or his father, for that matter. There were surely countless men that deserved praise, though not a one who deserved praise from God! These thoughts were running through his mind, but at the same time, his entire being was focused on the voice that continued to speak, and a physical feeling came over him that he was in a holy place.

"I will blot out man whom I have created from the face of the land, from man to animals to creeping things and to birds of the sky; for I am sorry that I have made them. The end of all flesh has come before me; for the earth is filled with violence because of them; and behold, I am about to destroy them with the earth."

Noah looked up slowly, raised his torso, and lifted his head toward the heavens while he was totally unconscious of any effort. He was moving but completely focused on the voice, the message. As God spoke, he felt a strength and ability that could have only come from his great Creator. He realized that God had not come to praise his humble servant but to recruit him.

The terror that should have seized him when the destruction of man was announced found no place in Noah's mind. God demanded his complete attention, and God *commanded* his complete attention! Like frozen moments in time, a series of pictures of the world and its wickedness ran through Noah's mind. Many of the impressions and visions were events and behaviors that he had seen with his very own eyes: the idol worship, praying to false gods, cursing the one true God and Creator, drunkenness, crimes, and evil practices of every sort.

Noah was not shown these things to convince him, but just as reminders of the world around him and what it had become. And Noah had not seen even a fraction of *all* the things God had witnessed among the people of the earth.

"Make for yourself an ark of gopher wood; you shall make the ark with rooms, and shall cover it inside and out with pitch. This is how you shall make it: the length of the ark three hundred cubits, its breadth fifty cubits, and its height thirty cubits. You shall make a window for the ark, and finish it to a cubit from the top; and set the door of the ark in the side of it; you shall make it with lower, second, and third decks."

The Lord God continued to describe what he would have Noah do. Noah was a man of the earth, not of the water. He was not an engineer or a craftsman, much less a builder of boats or ships. This ark would be enormous! Noah knew that a cubit was the distance from a man's elbow to the end of his hand (typically about 18 inches). This would make the vessel 450 feet long, seventy-five feet wide, and forty-five feet high! But it never crossed his mind to question the Lord's plan. It just seemed to sink in and was imbedded in his will. His only thought was, *Yes, my sovereign* Lord.

"Behold, I, even I am bringing the flood of water upon the earth, to destroy all flesh in which is the breath of life, from under heaven; everything that is on the earth shall perish. But I will establish my covenant with you; and you shall enter the ark—you and your sons and your wife, and your sons' wives with you."

Noah was on his knees but straight up and rigid with his face turned toward the heavens and his eyes closed tightly. There were visions just as moments earlier, and Noah could literally see this ark, the single door, the roof; he could see his wife, his sons, and their wives inside. It was as if he was seeing into the future, and as the LORD spoke to him, each detail became a vision. The visions had such clarity that Noah felt that he could have reached out and touched the ark; he could see the waters covering the earth. Even though Noah had no children, he could envision them in this ark.

As these revelations came to mind, he was not distracted by the details of all the things that surely should have raised so many questions. No man had ever seen some of the details God was describing, like water falling from the sky or bursting forth from the earth toward the heavens. All these things were being etched permanently into Noah's mind and on his heart.

"And of every living thing of all flesh, you shall bring two of every kind into the ark, to keep them alive with you; they shall be male and female. Of the birds after their kind, and of the animals after their kind, of every creeping thing of the ground after its kind, two of every kind will come to you to keep them alive. As for you, take for yourself some of all food which is edible, and gather it to yourself; and it shall be for food for you and for them."

Noah could envision every kind of animal on the earth coming to him, to this ark he was instructed to build. He could see these creatures as they moved, slowly but surely, in towards the opening in the side of the ark. Oddly enough, this one door seemed to be the only way in. The only way to their salvation through that door! This was the plan God was to provide for man and beast alike.

There was no fear in these animals. The herbivores were walking beside the carnivores. These animals had gathered in the immediate area surrounding the ark, and as if divinely guided, they moved into the structure in an orderly fashion. There were no stampedes or aggressive behavior. It was very unlike Noah's encounter with his fellow man when he had journeyed into the village some twenty years earlier. He could see himself standing at the entrance, calmly watching the orderly procession. He could see his wife, his sons, and their wives watching from atop the deck of the ark. No assistance was needed to get the creatures in. They were being ushered in by God. It was as if they understood there was only one way to their salvation, and they either chose it or perished in the waters.

Noah seemed to have lost all track of time. He had no idea how long he knelt there or how long the details of God's commission to him played over in his mind. He had envisioned each detail again and again, from the actual construction of the frame, the decks, and the window above, right up to the roof. He saw himself applying the pitch, sealing the inside and out. He saw the animals coming into the ark, which was already laden with provisions for them and the family he would bring inside.

Several hours had passed, and the sun had moved across the sky since he first heard God speak to him. Nothing had been accomplished in his field this day, but that didn't seem to matter. He rose to his feet, never noticing that his legs and knees were weakened from being in that position for so long. He dusted himself off half-heartedly, and little dust clouds drifted away as he swatted at his cloak. Then he stopped suddenly and quickly looked around in all directions. He looked into the sky again as he had first done this morning with a faint hope that he might glimpse his LORD disappearing into the heavens. But he was alone.

Noah did not doubt or question what he had heard and experienced. But as if to give this humble servant an extra dose of spiritual stamina, God placed his hand around Noah's shoulder and stood briefly gazing into the heavens with him. Tears again welled up in Noah's eyes, and a smile crossed his face as the renewed feeling of peace, strength, conviction, and praise for his LORD engulfed him. As they stood together, time seemed to stand still.

From their home, Metis noticed her husband standing alone in the field, staring off into the sky. She looked upwards to see what he might be looking at, but the sky was clear. There was nothing there. She was busy with her own feelings of thankfulness for having such a good man for a husband. He was such a caring companion and friend! She smiled at the lone figure and decided to go in and prepare the evening meal.

She turned to go back inside but then paused just briefly. She wondered if she might have turned too quickly, for her stomach suddenly felt a little queasy. It did not last more than a moment, and she forgot it had occurred almost as quickly as it had come upon her.

When Noah turned to head toward his home, his mind was racing. He was looking down at the ground as he walked and appeared to be in no hurry. He was figuring in his mind what he would need, how he would start, where he would start. He stopped and looked around again. Now, where would be a good place to build an ark? He pondered this for a moment, but this being his first ark, the answer did not come easily to him. The more he thought about it and all that would be involved, the more he realized how big the task was that was ahead of him! He figured he had better get an early start in the morning. He thought that perhaps his wife could help him decide where to build it. It would need to be close so he could start early and work late. Then it hit him. His wife had no idea what had happened to him today.

He looked toward his home and broke into a run, smiling as he ran. He had to tell her everything! Perhaps the praise he had received from God was due to her faithful, diligent prayers for him all these years. It surely wasn't because of anything he had done, he thought. He couldn't wait to see her face as he shared his experience in the fields with her.

THE ARK

Noah did everything just as God commanded him.

Genesis 6:22

Both Noah and Metis rose early the next morning, well before the sun. Neither of them could sleep any longer; they both felt very refreshed and energized. They got on their knees together inside their bedroom and prayed to God with a new sense of awe and gratitude they had never felt before. Even Metis prayed aloud this morning, thanking the LORD for the blessings and provisions he provided. And she prayed that he might watch over both of them as her husband set about doing God's bidding. She did not understand exactly what an ark was, though Noah had explained in detail, but she understood it meant salvation.

Noah prayed for guidance, wisdom, insight, and strength. He wanted his wife to think he understood perfectly what the LORD was having him build. But in reality, he was not a carpenter. He was not a boat builder, though this did not sound like any boat he had ever seen or heard about. It was to be huge! He wondered if the LORD had chosen the right person for this project. Noah rattled the dimensions off in his mind again, surprising himself that he could recall them so distinctly. Something of this size might take him most of the year! He too gave thanks for God's provision, past, present, and future.

As they prayed, they felt a peace come over them. It was so powerful it seemed physical. There was no doubt in their minds that God was in control and that they had nothing to be concerned about. When they had finished their time of prayer and worship, Metis began preparing breakfast. Noah walked outside in the front of their house and looked around.

Off in the western sky the stars were still shining brightly. Far off in the east, a sliver of pink and purple was slowly growing over the top of the hills stretching to the horizon as the dawn approached. From his vantage point high atop the crest of the hill where their home sat, he could see a good distance in all directions. As he admired the scenery all around him, his mind turned to the message the LORD had given him just yesterday. He could almost hear the words again, "This is how you shall make it: the length of the ark three hundred cubits, its breadth fifty cubits, and its height thirty cubits." He measured in his mind the area just before him in front of his house to the north.

He immediately realized there was no room to put it there. He began to study the areas to the east, west, and south of the home, but there was no way it was going to fit atop the hill. His fields were down the west side of the hill and into the flatlands beyond. The ridge of the hill continued to the south behind the home, but rock cropping and rugged terrain in that direction eliminated that possibility. The east was not wide enough before the ground sloped gently toward the beautiful valley below.

His eyes followed the slope of the ground down to the valley below. As his eyes reached the bottom, he felt something like a hand on his shoulder, a subtle comforting and reassuring touch. There was no one there, but Noah was not looking for anyone. The light from the rising sun had been steadily changing the colors behind the hills beyond the other side of the vale. Now, like angels of light, the sunlight raced across the floor of the valley, accenting its expanse. As Noah watched the spectacle God was providing, he was given the answer to his dilemma. The ark would be built in the valley below.

He studied the terrain. It was wide and level with large stands of trees bordering the open fields at the eastern and northern sides of the valley. To the south, the very ridge his house sat on curved from the west around the south end of the valley. A forest was established from the lowlands up the sides of the mount. It grew very dense at the top and went on for—Noah had no idea. He had wandered the forest up there and had not reached the other side that spread to the south. The Lord had provided the materials he would need.

Noah wandered down the incline and into the vale. He walked the area, admiring the evidence of his Creator but with another purpose in his mind. He surveyed the land, and as if given a divine revelation, he looked at his feet and turned completely around, widening his gaze. This was the spot! He looked back up the ridge to where his house sat. It would be no short journey each day, but he knew this was the very place where he would begin building the Lord's ark.

With that decision made, Noah headed back home. As he crested the hill, Metis met him, smiling broadly. "What has my husband been doing this fine blessed morning?" She threw her arms around him and gave him a big kiss on his cheek. He hugged her back tightly and then released her and turned with one arm still around her waist. She turned with him until they were both facing east, the new sun now well up over the crest of the hills on the horizon.

He waved his arm out over the valley below. "That is where God wants his ark built." He spoke with an unwavering certainty in his tone. She looked up at his profile and smiled. She knew her husband well enough to see that he was actually envisioning this ark even now, sitting in the valley. "This is going to be big," he whispered. They stood for a few moments more, and then, still with an arm about each other's waist, they turned together and went to their humble abode to share breakfast.

Immediately after he had eaten, Noah gathered his oxen and hitched them to their open-backed three-sided cart. He put his axe and other tools, the same ones he had used to construct the frame of his house, into the cart. He looked to his right down into his fields of crops and vineyards. He prayed for the LORD to keep the crops thriving while he was occupied with his new project. There was not a concern of the potential neglect or shortage of crops. The same peace they had been experiencing covered this circumstance also.

When he reached the bottom of the hill, he continued past the chosen location heading farther south and into the edge of the forest. As he approached and then began moving into the trees, he was sizing up a particular stand of trees he would start with. Without hesitation, he grabbed his axe and moved to the first tree and proceeded to chop it down. Then he removed all of the branches from the trunk. From there he moved to another and another until, as if being given divine direction, he paused and looked around at his work. Now he needed to get them to the building site. He took the cart with the tools to the building site and unhitched the oxen from the cart.

For the remainder of the day, he moved the trees from the forest to the building site one by one, staging them in ways that made no sense to him at the time. But he was being guided by the very wisdom and experience he had prayed for.

⸺

Noah stepped out of his small home and stretched. He raised his arms over his head, leaning from the waist as far as he could to the left and then to the right. He put his hands on his hips and leaned back at the waist, slight grunts coming out of his mouth with each movement. The cracking bones were the sound he was trying for, and he seemed satisfied with the results.

It was dark enough that the stars were still sprinkled about the heavens, shining brightly. Far away to the east, just at the horizon, he could see a difference in the color of the darkness. It was the birth of a new day. He looked out and observed his fields. Though they had been seriously neglected as of late, they seemed to be doing amazingly well. It was still too dark to see the individual plants, but he could see an outline of the areas, darker than the surrounding grounds.

Noah turned his attention from the crops to the valley below. He could see the silhouette of the foundation of the ark that he had been working on these past few months. He thought about what God would have him complete this day. He knelt and began to pray silently, giving thanks and praise for all the blessings in his life. He prayed an additional prayer for his wife and the baby she was carrying inside. Although he wasn't sure when his first child would come, he knew it would likely be very soon. It was getting harder for her to move around. But somehow everything still seemed to get done. Noah prayed that her days would be blessed and their child would be born healthy and strong.

There was a part of Noah that felt like he should be more supportive at home and spend less time away during the day. There were many things that she alone took care of around their home, and he knew he could lighten some of her burden. But she would not hear of it.

Noah recalled when he had come home that afternoon, out of breath and speaking so rapidly that she could barely understand what he was saying. Finally she grasped what he was trying to tell her and grew excited as she began to realize the vision. They talked all through the evening. There were many questions she had that Noah could not answer. There was fear and uncertainty in her questions and in her voice. So Noah told her all the Lord had said to him. That was what he had, and for him that was all he needed because it was God's message.

When they finally slept, which was very late, she slept peacefully. The Lord had spoken to her husband, and their faith in their God was more often than not as one. And since that time, she supported and encouraged his dedication to building the ark. She participated by bringing him meals and fresh water during the day while he worked.

When she had announced to Noah that she was with child,

she insisted that he continue to focus on God's work and to make that his priority. The LORD would make sure they did not want during this time as long as they remained faithful. As their child grew in her womb, more and more Noah would ask if he should stay home or come home early. She could see in his eyes that he was torn between caring for her and doing the LORD's work. It was not that he was putting her above God; she understood that. It was just as she did not put her husband above the LORD. But he worried that she may be working too hard. And he knew before he asked these questions what her response would be. She would send Noah off to do God's work, telling him not to worry about her; she was fine. And the LORD blessed her in those days.

He prayed for the LORD to guide his hands, thoughts, and heart each day. He had no clue about how to build something like the ark, but each day he went down to the site he had chosen and the day's work just came to him. At the end of each day as he walked back to his home, he would turn and look down upon the frame slowly taking shape below. It amazed him that he had accomplished the things he had in such a short time. It was still only a partial frame, not much in relation to what it would be. But Noah could envision the vessel taking shape and form and was comfortable that all he had accomplished was just as it needed to be.

He prayed for the earth and the people in it. But the LORD had been very specific about the passengers on this ark that were to be saved from the great flood. Noah, his wife, his sons, and their wives were the only humans to go into the ark. He wondered about his father, his grandfather, and their other children. Not all of them walked with God, but surely Lamech and Methuselah had not fallen so far away from him. Some of these questions puzzled him, but he would not question the LORD's plan and his perfect justice.

Noah also considered all of the other people who roamed the earth. Most of them Noah would never meet. He knew that most of those he had come in contact with were consumed by evil and their wicked ways. As he prayed, he tried to keep his mind away from the things they did or said or spoke of. He wanted no part of it. But he prayed earnestly for their souls. And he prayed, above all else, that the LORD's will be done. Noah knew that the LORD's ways, thoughts, and deeds were not his and not of this world. He prayed to understand more than he did. He also prayed that he would not become caught in the trap of trying to compare the Creator of all things to the standards of this earth, particularly not *this* earth.

He prayed that he would leave those things to God that needed to be handled by God and that he would be blessed to understand what God desired him to do each day.

When he had finished praying, he rose silently and gathered his tools and the skin of water he took each morning. He looked back over one shoulder to his fields. The rising sun, though still hidden beneath the distant horizon, had lightened things a little more. He could see the plants of his field a little better now, and it really looked like the best crop he had seen in many years! He laughed to himself as he turned back and began to make his way to the ark. "I should have abandoned the fields long ago," he joked. "They seem to do much better without my tender care." And then he gazed upwards, giving the LORD silent but sincere praise, worshipping him and thanking him again for taking such good care of his crops, his wife, and their humble home.

Day after day, Noah started his mornings the same way. He rose early before the sun rose in the sky, and after he had spent some time with God, he would eat a brief morning meal. Then he would go down to the ark and work until after the sun had set. Often, though not each day, his wife would come down to spend some time watching him work and offering to help. Sometimes she would assist by just carrying smaller things like tools or pegs from one place to another. And other times she would help by making the holes in the beams and logs to take the pegs that would hold the various pieces together. She did not ask many questions about why something was done or how something would be done or what might come next. She discovered very early on that her husband could not answer most of her questions. He simply did not know, for God had not revealed it to him. But as he moved around the site, putting pieces into place and moving to the next section, it all just seemed to come together.

When she became heavy with child, she would not journey far from the house; it was just too hard. During the day when she had quiet time, she liked to sit in the shade of their home and watch Noah working in the distance. She saw the huge floor of the ark beginning to take shape and smiled as her husband moved about over the form, never seeming to stop or slow down.

She worried a little about Noah's massive undertaking. She needed to remind herself whom he was working for. God had told Noah to build this ark so that they would be saved. These thoughts would ease her mind again. God's promise was good enough for her; her husband would be just fine.

On this day, Noah was atop the developing deck. It was like a giant rectangle placed on the floor of the valley below the house. He was measuring the dimensions of the form again. He carefully laid the rod at the front edge and marked each section as he moved across. He had done this so many times that there were already marks where he had verified his dimensions. But as the deck grew, he checked his work more often to be sure he did all things just as the Lord had commanded. "300 cubits by 50 cubits by 30 cubits." The words resounded in his ears just as he remembered hearing them on that day, the day God spoke to him.

He paused when he reached the outer edge of the front end of the deck and was very satisfied that the measurements were just as God had required. He looked from the edge of the floor of the deck and slowly turned his eyes upward and envisioned the thirty cubits height the ark would eventually be. He had not even started the sides yet. In fact, there was still so much remaining to get the bottom shape completed according to God's plan that it would be some time before he would see any height to this mass.

Rather than feeling totally overwhelmed by the work that

remained, Noah looked at it from the point of view of, "Well, if I don't get back to work, it will never get done." He realized that this was going to be occupying his days for a very long time.

He remembered the LORD saying, "You and your sons and your wife and your sons' wives with you." His first son was not even born yet, not to mention him having a wife. But the LORD said "sons," more than one! He smiled to himself, thinking of his sons. He thought so often as he worked about raising these sons that he hoped would love, obey, and follow God all the days of their lives. He prayed he could do as his father and his grandfather had done by passing on this legacy to the next generation.

<hr>

When he finally trudged up the hill to his home that evening, he was feeling tired and sore but very pleased with his progress for the day. He could almost feel the angel supporting him as he made his way up the path he had worn between the valley below and their house on the hill. He paused as the path leveled out at the top of the incline to look over the fields below on the opposite side of the hill. He was so tired! He shook his head and thought, *That will have to wait for another day.*

Already it was too dark to see the condition of the field and vineyards. He could just make out the silhouettes of the vegetation but no details of their condition. He turned toward the house saying a silent prayer to God to take care of the crops while he was otherwise occupied.

Then his thoughts turned to Metis. He seemed to get a small burst of energy as he thought of his wife inside, most likely with a meal prepared for him. Even though she was so large she had trouble moving around, she insisted on having things ready for Noah when he came home. She told him he needed to rest after a long hard day and should not be worrying about having to fix meals just because she was "a little uncomfortable," to use her words. He truly loved her so much!

It was then he realized that she was not at the door to greet him with her captivating smile. He moved a little quicker the last few yards to the doorway, opened it, and stepped in. A dim light of an oil lamp shining from the room where they slept was the only light in the house. It was dark, but he could clearly see that his wife was not out in the front room. He went to the bedroom, and as he grasped both sides of the door and looked in, she turned from the bed to see a worried look on her husband's face.

"Metis?" He rushed to her side and knelt beside her. Her forehead was wet from sweat, and he looked around for something to wipe her brow. "Are you okay?" He felt a little silly asking the question because she certainly did not look okay. But that was all that would come to him as his mind created all sorts of possibilities, none that he felt equipped to do anything about.

She put her hand on his right shoulder. Then she reached up and turned his face toward hers. "I'm fine," she assured him. "It's just time for Japheth to come meet his father. He's tired of my stories and songs every day." She smiled at her husband, who did not seem to be handling this well at all. "He wants his father to tell him about this awesome God he serves."

Noah's eyes got larger with the realization that the baby was coming. "Shouldn't there be other people here?" His mind raced trying to think of who might be close enough to reach them quickly. There was no one, but that was not the answer he was looking for. "What will we—" His sentence was cut off when she clenched his shoulder and her whole body became rigid. She was in serious pain, but she found herself nearly laughing at her husband. She had not thought his eyes could get any larger than they were the moment he realized the baby was coming. But now she was sure his eyes had doubled in size when he saw her in pain.

A moment later the pain subsided, but Noah was petrified. Metis had never had a child herself before, but she had been around many women who had. She knew she needed to get her husband busy—and quickly. "Noah!" She yelled to make him focus on her words, not her circumstances. "We will need water and cloths, plenty of both." She put her hand on his cheek. His eyes softened as her touch seemed to tell him everything would be fine. "Can you get them together for me?"

Noah stood up quickly to start the tasks he had been given, but he stopped short and looked back at his wife. "Are you sure I should leave you?"

She nodded, smiled, and closed her eyes. "Yes. Noah, the pains will keep coming faster and harder. That is normal." She reached up for his hand, and he reached down and took hers softly. At that moment, another contraction started. It came fast and it was hard. She squeezed Noah's hand as the intensity increased. He was surprised at the strength of the small woman lying there. He knelt back at her side until the contraction subsided and the deep breaths she was taking slowly returned to normal. She held to his hand a while after the contraction was over. She thought how strong, rugged, and calloused that hand was from doing God's work.

She looked at him again. "This is normal, my love," she tried to assure him. "I need you to take over and get things ready, the water and the cloths. As the pains get closer, they will get harder, and I may not be able to tell you everything that needs to be done." Noah tried to listen intently, but it was hard to see her suffering like this. She continued, "This is how it is with all women. Except we have God's promise of sons. We already know he has plans for you and me and our children. Remember his promises when it gets difficult."

Noah smiled back at his wife. He knew there was nothing to be concerned about. "I'll be back soon!" He jumped up and rushed to the outer room to get water he had brought in from this morning for his wife before he had left. He gathered some in a clay pitcher and gathered the cloths he could find. He felt like he was taking an eternity. When another contraction would come, he would wince as he heard her groans. He prayed as he had never prayed before. He prayed reminding God of his promises, but Noah knew that was not really necessary.

It was a very long night for both Metis and Noah, but before the dawn, Japheth was resting in his mother's arms. Metis thought to herself, *That went rather well.* Beside her bed, Noah was in a sitting position, his feet and legs folded under his torso with his head resting on her left shoulder. He was snoring loudly. She looked back and forth between her new son and her husband. Then she closed her eyes, giving thanks and praise to the God she had come to know, love, and serve. She was certainly feeling blessed.

Noah did not go down to the ark for the next few days but did whatever he could to help until his wife was up and around. Even then he only returned to his task at her insistence that she was fine and able to take care of things while he was away during the day. Then he would come home early each day for a couple of weeks. He told his wife it was to check on her. She knew that was part of it, but she suspected he also wanted to spend time with his new son. And she thought that was wonderful.

Noah diligently continued building the ark, taking care to keep all the details as the LORD commanded. This day, he was in the forest gathering trees and hauling them to the work site. His oxen could easily drag the logs once the branches had been removed. He would gather several at one time near the site and then concentrate on shaping, cutting, and planning for the next step of the design. The design had been placed in his mind by the LORD, and it was as though it was being released to him a little at a time.

Noah was still in awe of the skills he had been given to accomplish this magnificent work. Shem walked at the head of the oxen team as they dragged the huge logs out of the forest, heading back to their destination. Ham and Japheth walked beside their father, trailing behind the oxen and their load. In the years since they had been born, Noah spent more time in prayer each morning and evening, thanking the LORD for such a blessed family.

Japheth, whose name meant "opened," was his oldest son. Shem, whose name meant "name, reputation, memory, or renown," and Ham, whose name meant "hot," were born one after the other, in almost rapid succession. Noah and his wife had gone from no children, just a promise from God for sons, to a family of three boys in what seemed almost no time at all.

The boys were eager to help their father and to learn all he had to teach them. And they learned much more about building than Noah knew at their ages. He had not had much experience, especially on something like the ark. But as the techniques and methods were revealed to Noah, his sons were there to see, observe, and learn throughout their youth. They loved to hear their father tell them about God and all the things he had done.

When they observed the world around them, the simple things like a leaf, a tree, a butterfly, or a fish, they would study them intently, in awe of the way they were made. They were discovering that each thing was created so differently, serving a unique purpose on God's earth. They were very curious boys, asking questions about anything and everything. And Noah beamed as he thought of how quickly they were learning.

Ham and Japheth were asking their usual multitude of questions when Noah noticed that Shem had halted the oxen just ahead. He stood there staring out to the edge of the woods. When Noah stopped, the other two boys also stopped in mid-step and mid-question.

"Father," Shem looked back to the others behind as he held tight to the oxen, "there are visitors coming." He spoke almost quietly; in his heart he dreaded the exchange between the strangers and his father. They all walked slowly to where Shem stood. Shem and his brothers had witnessed many encounters with curious visitors, and most were not pleasant. Noah looked out into the valley where the ark lay, like the foundation of some palace in its early stages of construction. A short distance away to the east, a small caravan of travelers was making its way toward the valley where the ark lay. Very likely, it was headed toward the village where Noah had saved the man many years ago. He felt a little uneasy about the fact that these travelers could not help but notice the ark, given the current direction they were traveling. They were still about half a mile away, but so were Noah and his sons.

"Why don't we just stay up here and let them have a look around and be on their way?" Shem asked. His eyes met his father's, and he knew the answer before Noah spoke.

"No, I can't let them keep us from our work. It is better that I greet them and try to tell them about the one true God. If I don't, they may never have an opportunity to hear truth." Noah looked into his son's eyes directly. He knew the pain that Shem felt for him. Many times he faced ridicule and laughter from these lost souls. "We can't make them believe, but I must try to reach them. I also must be sure they do not go bother your mother at home." He looked to the other side of the valley to their home resting atop a hill. "If we hide here and they decide to go that way, we could not reach her in time to ensure her safety. We do not know these people."

After Noah took a brief moment to ponder the situation, he decided to greet the travelers alone and leave his sons safely hidden. It was a shady spot, and he had carried a small bag of food and a skin of water for them that morning. He gave the food and water to them and gave instructions not to come out of the forest until he returned for them. He felt it was better to err on the side of caution rather than expose the boys to this group of strangers. More than likely, they would simply pass by and there would be nothing more to talk about. But Noah looked at the ark ahead, and just its size out in the middle of nowhere couldn't help but draw attention.

Shem knew the responsibility his father felt, carrying the message from God about the fate of everyone. He seemed to understand it better than Japheth and Ham.

"Can we go with you, Father?" Ham asked excitedly. He liked it when visitors came. He liked stories of the places beyond their home. "They might tell us more stories of the cities and kingdoms far from here!" He did not try to contain his excitement even though he knew his father did not care for the world beyond. "Let's go and greet them!"

"I'll go myself." Noah turned to study the face of his youngest. Ham immediately looked dejected. He turned his eyes away and down. He secretly hoped his father might see his sadness and change his mind. "You boys stay here and keep hidden in the trees." Noah hoped that his trek down to the ark would not be noticed by the party still in the distance. He prayed they would not arrive until well after he got to the structure below. Japheth was already looking around to determine where he would go exploring. He was familiar with the woods and spent much of his free time wandering them. Noah knew he would need to be on his way if he planned to get there before the strangers arrived.

"Be careful." Shem touched his father's arm as Noah turned to leave.

"Don't worry, son." Noah smiled back at his eldest. "God has not taken me this far to have something happen now. He has promised."

"Yes, I know, Father." Shem already felt better. Sometimes in the daily goings on, Shem needed to be reminded of God's promises. "God will protect you." He turned towards Ham and Japheth, who were both preoccupied with other things. Noah started off toward the building site.

Ham huffed and his shoulders sank low. "Why couldn't I go with him and you two could stay here?" He looked at Shem. "Just because you are afraid of a stranger doesn't mean I have to be." He was a little angry at Shem. If his brother had sided with him, he felt they may have been able to go meet the strangers. He turned toward Japheth, who was now wandering back into the forest. "When I am old enough to be on my own, I'll build a great city that everyone will want live in. Everyone will want to come visit me," he muttered under his breath, but Shem had already heard it too many times not to know what his brother said.

"Don't go far!" Shem called after Japheth. He meant it for Ham also. He could not leave the oxen, and with their load, he could not easily turn them and follow his brothers. He wanted to keep an eye on his father anyway. He felt uneasy about strangers. To him, these were people who had been condemned by their lifestyle. What did they have to lose at this stage?

Japheth looked behind him and saw Ham coming toward

him. "I thought you would want to watch the strangers." Japheth jeered at his brother. Japheth loved the outdoors and open country, forests, mountains, fields, and valleys. He marveled at the nature around him, often in awe of all God's creation. "Surely you don't want to see the boring trees and wildlife around here, do you?"

"The trees aren't boring." Ham tried to sound uninterested in his brother's taunts. "You are the boring one. I'd much rather be hearing about the great cities and kingdoms out there," he waved his arm out toward and beyond the valley, "than watching you frolic in the forest." If he could get Japheth to go with him, he wanted to sneak down to the ark. He would not go alone, but if he could find an accomplice, his father might not be as angry when they were caught.

An eagle screamed overhead as it glided on the currents high about the canopy. Japheth was immediately drawn to the scene above. Ham looked up but not with the same sense of awe that Japheth had. "Only God could create such things!" Japheth watched as the bird hovered on the currents directly above him. He looked at Ham and smiled as he saw the attention even his skeptical brother gave the display. Japheth dropped to one knee and silently gave thanks to the LORD.

Ham turned to face his brother. A twinge of guilt went through him as he realized that he focused more on the world around him than he did the Creator. He loved his family and the way of life he was being taught. He was young, but he understood that it was this way of life that would put him among the saved when God judged the world. His father tried to convince others that they were on a path to destruction, but they always just considered him a lunatic. He loved his father for not giving up on them. He wondered what his father might think of his desire to be in the cities and villages he had only heard about. It didn't sound so wicked when he heard strangers talk of where they came from.

Ham looked back at Shem, who was watching Japheth. It made him smile to think how blessed he really was with this family. His father's encouragement to worship came back to him, and he joined Japheth on his knees. Together they praised and gave thanks to the sovereign LORD. Ham forgot about trying to sneak down to the ark any longer.

As Noah neared the building site, he saw the caravan that had stopped just ahead. They were looking in the direction of the huge deck, no doubt, just as Noah had assumed; they were trying to determine what it was and what it was doing here. Curiosity got the better of them, and when one of the men atop a camel spotted Noah, he announced it to the others. Immediately they turned towards the great structure (though still only a large, thick deck) and made their way to the site.

Noah busied himself with small housekeeping tasks, killing time until they arrived. He did not stare at them or direct his attention to them until they had nearly arrived. But all the while he was aware of their progress. When he did stop his work, he walked toward the front of the ark and waved to them. Some of them waved back, but several of them were carrying loads, burdens they were carrying in addition to the things piled high on the camels and donkeys. Noah figured these must be slaves.

One man in particular seemed to be the leader of this group. He was dressed in the best robes and garments. He was adorned with gaudy jewelry, and his haughtiness told Noah that this stranger was quite taken with himself! He was a very plump man who had a big smile across his face as he approached. Greetings were exchanged; the man was loud and very animated, hugging Noah like a long lost brother. He threw out his name along with a few others, describing himself as a humble merchant in search of a village he knew to be nearby.

Noah took this opportunity to point him in the direction of the village and gave him an approximate distance to his destination. A part of him hoped they might just continue on. The men in the caravan that he assumed to be slaves had lowered their burdens to the ground and just stood still, watching the others. A few others, whether fellow merchants or perhaps even relatives Noah did not know, began to poke around, quite curious about what was being built here.

The deck was nearly as thick as they were tall, though it

stood up on piers that Noah had put in the ground to support the frame and keep it directly off the soil below. But even so, it was easily three cubits thick. Noah continued talking with the man before him but watched every move of the others who were exploring. He did not try to follow them out of the corner of his eye but watched them directly, his head moving with their movements along the outer edge of the frame. But they were simply curious, actually pretty amazed.

With greetings and pleasantries out of the way, the merchant who was adorned with the gaudy jewelry finally turned the discussion to the object of their curiosity.

"My brother!" he began. "We have detoured from our path to come and praise your efforts here! What a glorious temple this will be, a beacon to the poor souls crossing this land! The tired and weary, despondent from their tedious journey…then behold! A temple to the god, of, umm, what god is this temple dedicated to?"

The merchant was leaning so far to his left trying to get Noah's attention that he was in serious danger of falling over. He was trying to look into Noah's face, but Noah had turned away to keep an eye on the other men, still wandering about the structure. They had paused when they heard mention of a temple and the inquiry of the god to which this temple was being built. When they looked at the men at the front of the ark, they saw Noah watching their every move. His stare seemed locked on them, and immediately they felt uneasy. Sensing they were not where they should be, they started walking back towards Noah and the merchant.

"It's not a temple." Noah never took his eyes off of the other men who tried to smile at him as they came around the front of the structure.

"Not a temple?" The merchant looked puzzled. He was certain that was what this man was building. Then, as if a light went off in his mind, the puzzled look was replaced by his big, captivating grin. No doubt this grin had served him well over the years in his business of trading and negotiations. "Ah ha!" he said, satisfied with himself. "You are building a palace for a king or perhaps a rich prince in a nearby kingdom." He was trying to cover his bases after the first miscalculation.

"It's not a palace," Noah said dryly, now turning to face the merchant since the other travelers were where he could keep an eye on them.

"Then, brother, I am truly perplexed." The merchant raised his eyebrows, actually looking sadly puzzled. "What exactly *is* being built here and where are the workers? Surely a man of your intellect is the overseer of the workforce. I would have thought to see them quite busy this time of day."

"I am the worker," Noah said. He was feeling better now that all of the travelers were close together where he could watch them.

"I don't understand! You are the worker, you alone?" The merchant looked into Noah's eyes to try to detect something that might give away the explanation, the true purpose, the meaning of this large object in the middle of nowhere.

"Yes, I alone am doing God's work here."

"Yes! I knew it!" The merchant practically shouted looking back to his companions for acknowledgement of his wisdom and discernment. On cue, they nodded and grinned and bowed their heads quickly up and down. "I knew this was a temple! Which god is it for?" he asked.

Noah looked deep into the man's eyes. "I work for the one true God, the *only God*." Noah's eyes narrowed and he leaned closer, his eyebrows furrowing, trying to impress his point to these pagans. "There are no other gods before him or after him."

"One god?" The merchant started laughing. "My poor lost fellow! If there is only one god, tell me, what is he god of? Is he god of the stars? Then who is god of the moon? Is he god of the water? Then who is god of the vine?" Still chuckling, he turned to his companions, who were chuckling also. "Only one god indeed. That is preposterous."

Noah realized that though the men were laughing, they were completely serious. These men truly felt there must be a different god for everything they saw and everything that happened in their lives. The merchant turned back to Noah and put his hand on his shoulder. "Tell me, my brother, what is this temple for? I will help you identify the god so you do not offend him with your ignorance."

"It's not a temple. It is an ark." Noah felt sorry for the men.

"A what? An ark? What, pray tell us, is an ark?"

Noah looked the man right in the eyes, and without hesitation he said, "It is the salvation for the earth. When God destroys the earth, only the people and creatures in this ark will survive. When the flood comes, nothing outside of the ark will remain alive."

"Yes, yes. I see now, you have had a vision. Okay. Let's see, a flood." The merchant looked around for a moment, and then a sad and sorrowful look came upon his face. "My poor fellow, there is no body of water in this vicinity nearly large enough to flood this land. Your heart is right to worship the god of the waters, but he will never see your monument to him so far from the places he would reign." He moved beside Noah and put his arm across Noah's shoulder. "Abandon this folly and travel to a place where you will be near the water and see if this god calls you again. If you are so called, build your monument there. We will pray to the water god to bless you, my friend. Tell us his name that we may pray more effectively." The other men solemnly nodded in agreement with the merchant.

Noah stepped back from the merchant, put his hand on the man's shoulder, and again looked deep into his eyes. "Pray for yourselves, brother. You will be among those who perish in the flood. The one true God is the LORD. He is Creator of everything that is, was, or ever will be. He has seen the wickedness of man. He has heard your prayers to the nonexistent gods you worship. He knows your rejection of him. He is a patient and loving God who desires to see his children turn from their evil ways. But he will not tolerate your rejection forever. He will not allow your wickedness to go unpunished forever!"

The men standing behind the merchant were shocked. Their eyes and mouths were opened wide. But the merchant's eyes had been narrowing as Noah spoke until they were like slits on his face. He was not smiling now. He sneered at the man who dared to call him wicked. He knew that his multitude of gods could override any curse or judgment this crazy man's solitary god could throw at them.

He felt somewhat sorry for the wild delusions of the man before him. But this fool was on his own now. He had insulted and embarrassed him in front of his entourage. "We will see whose god prevails, my friend," he whispered. He backed away slowly and began waving his hands in quick motions at the men who traveled with him. Those with loads began picking them up, making themselves ready to leave. He looked directly at Noah and gave him his advice. "For your own safety, abandon this project. It will draw attention that I am certain you neither want nor need. Others may not be as gracious as I." His eyes softened a little as he looked toward the home atop the hill in the distance. "Do it for them."

Noah prayed for these men as they moved away, turning in the direction of the village. The man's warning was sincere, but he was lost in his world. Nothing Noah could have said would break through to him. But he knew from the faces of the two young men in the group, perhaps this merchant's sons, they had much to think about. But where they were going, they had no hope of receiving guidance to any place but destruction.

Noah started to go after them and invite them to stay. But the angel at his side put his hand on Noah's arm and stopped him. In that moment, Noah knew they would not abandon the life they knew. For the remainder of their years, they would be blown this way and that with each new idea that would be presented to them. They would change gods as often as some change garments.

When they had disappeared behind the first hill, Noah turned back toward the forest where his boys were waiting. They had remained in the shade of the trees, hidden from the caravan of men. Shem had watched everything below though he could not hear what was being said. He was not afraid, just very curious. Ham and Japheth watched with him some of the time, but for the most part they played and roughhoused and enjoyed the cool of the forest canopy.

Shem saw his father heading back toward them. He then turned to watch his brothers lying quietly now in the grass, watching the sky through the tops of the trees. Behind them, an angel had stood the entire time Noah was gone, patiently guarding the boys from anything that might want to harm them. They had been totally unaware of the wolf pack that paused out of sight and gave this area a wide berth. Something suggested they stay away. They never saw the bear on his way through that also changed course because of the aura around that place. Nothing was to happen to Noah's family, and God saw to that.

Noah greeted the boys, who were excited to see him again. As they started down the path together with Shem leading the oxen, Noah told his sons one more time about their awesome God. There were lots of questions about the visitors, so he told them of the men's confusion. They were seeking happiness in this world, but not seeking God, and they would never have the peace they sought.

After a productive day doing God's work, they returned home. Noah told his wife all about the visitors. She was very interested in the details since she had watched the encounter from the safety of their little home. The family prayed that night, giving thanks and praise to God. And they prayed for the lost souls who had chanced upon them that day.

As the boys grew older, Noah gave them more and more responsibilities. He trained them in the various tasks that he had been given divine instruction to learn himself. He did not have the skills or knowledge to do this work when he started. But God had provided exactly what skills he needed when he needed it at the various stages of development for the ark. Many days Noah would step back to look over the things accomplished that day and would be in awe of his God more and more.

"What is this called again, Father?" Ham asked as he held up the plane he was shaping a piece of wood with.

Noah noticed that Ham seemed more interested in the details of each task he was given. "That is an adze," he responded.

Ham looked it over carefully, studying the way it was made. "Adze," he repeated more to himself as he went back to work. Noah had responded to similar questions with each new task or tool. "Why are we making these sides flat? Why do we have to cut notches in the ends?" Sometimes the questions seemed never-ending, but Noah did not mind. He could see his youngest son soaking up the information as it was passed on.

Ham would go back over areas where they had fitted beams together looking closely at the finished work or running his hand over it studying the textures it would seem. "I will take this knowledge with me when I build great cities and buildings," he would say to himself, daydreaming of kingdoms he would build. But he kept these things to himself and did not openly share them with his brothers nor his mother or father.

Japheth, on the other hand, could not seem less interested in the why or how. He enjoyed working with his father and helping wherever he could. He was strong, even at an early age. His father was surprised at the hours of work his son could put in, even doing very tedious labor, but still have the energy to take off into the woods once they were done. He would spend hours alone there following the animals. He could move silently through the densest forest following fox, wolves, bears, or whatever without them seeing or hearing him. He did not know that God had angels with him at all times watching and protecting.

Japheth loved his father and mother, and he loved the trees, animals, and birds around him. He would often give thanks to God, just as his father had done time after time. And he would inquire about other things. "Why don't those people believe that God is the one true God?" he often asked after strangers or visitors left. It puzzled him how his father could explain so clearly and show them the evidence that no one could deny all around them every day, but still they would leave either laughing or angry. It seemed the visitors found it easier to make up a multitude of gods to pray to in vain. "What will happen to those people when the ark is finished?" Japheth asked his father.

"God will turn his back on them just as they have rejected him." Noah did not say more, but Japheth knew this was not a good thing.

Shem, Noah's second son, was more like Japheth than he was like Ham. However, he did not share the same passion for the nature around him that his older brother had. He loved being outdoors and the animals fascinated him, but he was one more to be in awe of the Creator rather than worshipping the creation.

He paid close attention to the tasks he might be assigned at the ark, and it was rare that instruction had to be given more than once. He was one who did his work, did not say a lot, but took some pride in doing a good and thorough job.

Over the next few decades, the ark began to really take shape. As Shem, Ham, and Japheth grew into strong young men, their skills increased daily. As the design of the ark was revealed to Noah, he passed it on to his sons, and they gained great skills, which they never forgot.

Noah gave thanks each day for the LORD guiding every step of this vast project. At the end of each day, the four of them would stop as they neared their home to look back down over the ark below. Even though his sons were becoming very skilled as they learned more and more, they all marveled at the LORD's work sitting below them taking shape little by little. The deck had been completed, and the beams for the sides had been put in. The middle and upper decks had been framed in, and gradual ramps between the floors had been completed. They were the primary access between the floors of the ark, which was about forty-five feet (thirty cubits) high.

Now that they were older, Noah could send his sons into the forest on their own to gather trees and wood for the ark. He typically would continue working with one of his sons while the other two would go together to gather materials. And in this way the work progressed much quicker than it had when Noah was working alone.

Noah was very proud of their work. He beamed with pride as he observed their labor. They never complained nor did they avoid the duties given them by their father each day. They would gather in the afternoon to have a small meal their mother would provide; she would eat with them and they would talk.

As his sons grew into men, Noah greatly enjoyed their talks together. They talked about such things as God's faithfulness, the work they were doing, and so many other things that pertained to their lives. It was encouraging to Noah to see these men grow in wisdom and stature, loving the LORD as they did.

On occasion Noah thought about the first visitors to the ark so many years ago; they were convinced this was a temple. Noah supposed in some ways it was. He never had trouble giving praise to God when he was working here. He and his sons could sense the LORD guiding them each step of the way, each beam, each stud, and each rafter that was put into place.

There had been many other visitors since that first caravan happened by. It was obvious that the first caravan had spread the word of Noah's undertaking. Though they had probably shared their encounter with Noah only in the village, it was obvious to him that word had spread far beyond that about the great temple in the wilderness. Some came to worship; some came just to see if it was true. Some stopped and watched at a distance, and some came to Noah to ask questions and see what this was all about.

Those who inquired about details to Noah were sorry they ever had! He was all too happy to talk about his great God and his faithfulness. His sons would continue to work as their father told these curiosity seekers exactly what this was and why it was here. And he told them why the LORD was going to destroy them all.

From above, Noah's sons would grin at one another as Noah began his explanations. They had grown accustomed to the distractions, and they marveled at the variety of reactions to their father's message. Some swore they would repent and beginning that very day their lives would change. Some became enraged that a stranger would dare tell them they were wicked and evil. Some would laugh and ridicule the men for taking on such a foolish and monumental task.

But they were never aware of the multitudes of people that headed out to the site with different motives that never arrived. Angels would turn them this way and that, confusing their directions and distorting the landscape in their eyes, so much so that they were forced to give up and go home. Some had in mind to destroy the work in the wilderness and put a stop to this crazy man and his high and mighty position. But they either never made it to the site or forgot why they came when they finally did arrive. And after they were insulted by the crazy man informing them of the ungodly things (they knew) they were doing, they would leave, only to become enraged the next day over the turn of events.

There were times Noah felt the interruptions were too much, so he would continue his work and simply ignore the disturbance altogether. He was given a sense of urgency that seemed stronger at times to continue his work rather than deal with the visitors. At these times, no matter how much calling or pleading came from below, Noah would ignore the strangers and continue his work. At times, one of his sons would go down and encourage them to leave. And they left disappointed that the crazy man in the wilderness had not entertained them that day.

During harvest time, Noah assigned two of his sons to bring in the crops while he and his third son continued to work on the ark. Noah varied the duties of his sons so that each of them would learn all that he could. Noah tried to be fair to his sons so that they never felt like they were being mistreated by being assigned to the chores they did not care for.

Japheth seemed to take to land more than his two brothers. And he found a satisfaction in working the ground that his father had known before he embarked on building the ark. Noah noticed this, so he placed Japheth in charge of the crops; he was the overseer of the family food source.

Because God was blessing Noah and his family, food was never scarce in these times. The sheep and goats grew fat and multiplied. They were allowed to roam the countryside unattended, and they never strayed very far. The LORD watched over them; he kept them safe from predators and the elements so the men could focus on his work.

NOAH'S SONS' WIVES

But I will establish my covenant with you, and you
will enter the ark—you and your sons and your
wife and your sons' wives with you.

Genesis 6:18

Noah stood outside of his home, just as he had done so many
times in the past few centuries. But this day was different from
all the others. It was particularly different from the days of the
past several decades. This day, Noah would not be going down
to work on the ark. Noah's sons, Shem, Ham, and Japheth, were
not on their way to work on the ark either. The sun was high
up in the sky, but they had not been to the building site at all
this day.

This was a very special day. Actually, this day was the beginning of a number of days for celebration. The family was
expecting company. They would start arriving at any time. In
fact, Noah was on lookout to see if anyone was drawing near.
The company would continue to arrive over the next few days.
Noah gazed into the distance, anxiously looking for indication
of movement in the direction of his humble home. No, nothing yet.

The ark was not being abandoned, as had been recommended by so many unwelcome and uninvited visitors over the years. They were taking a break for a wedding! Noah grinned to himself, standing there alone. His sons, who were now grown men, were getting married. It had all been arranged for some time. The brides had been selected, and arrangements with the families had been made. Rooms had been added to the small home the sons had grown up in; there was one for each of them.

Noah and his wife would welcome the additional hands around the house. There would be the companionship for Noah's wife while the men were out working each day. It would be more mouths to feed, but there had been no lack of resources around this home since the building of the ark had begun so many years ago. So Noah did not concern himself with any lack of provisions for his family. Everyone in the home understood that the LORD always provided for his children.

With the LORD's blessing, there would be children to follow these new marriages. Noah thought to himself that he would have the beginnings of his own tribe. He thought about that for a moment and then remembered the LORD's words to him. His tribe, these new brides, his sons, and his wife would be all of the people remaining on the earth once the flood was over.

Contrary to what many scoffers and nonbelievers tried to tell him, Noah never doubted that the LORD would do exactly as he had told him. The cynics who tried to discourage him would point out that he had been building this thing for over fifty years. Thank goodness, they told him, that God was not true to his word. If he had been, Noah's family would have been destroyed with everyone else.

They would laugh at him, ridicule him, and curse at him for his misguided faith, as they called it.

But Noah knew that the LORD was being patient not only with Noah but also with the rest of humanity in the unlikely event that they would turn from their wicked ways. But their behavior grew more depraved as time passed.

Noah knew these young women who came to marry his sons actually had come from good families. But that didn't always provide the assurance that the children of good people would not turn away from God. There was so much influence from the world, and it seemed there were far too few voices to share God's love, his mercy and glory. For those who were occupied with the things of the world couldn't see the evidence of God all around them.

Noah wondered about his own family: his father, his grandfather, and those that had passed on since he was a young man. When he was just eighty-four, Enosh, his grandfather's great-great-great-grandfather, had passed away at the age of 905. Since that time, Enosh's son Kenan had passed away when Noah was just 179 years old. Then Mahalalel and Jared, his grandfather's great-grandfather and grandfather, had passed away. Each of these men had left many children who had many more children of their own.

So many of these relatives Noah had never met, and many of them the family did not speak of. Perhaps they did not speak of them because of the distances away and the time since they had last seen or heard from them. Or perhaps it was because of the life they had chosen.

His own father and grandfather had children after Noah's birth; many of these family members had grown up and moved away to start lives of their own. Noah often prayed about the choices his aunts, uncles, brothers, and sisters had made. If they were not following God, he prayed for him to reach them and help them choose wisely.

"The earth is filled with violence because of them." The Lord's words echoed in his ears. Along with his relatives, Noah considered the strangers and faceless people who were coming to mind. Over the years, the truth for him had come to light. Many of his relatives were among those that filled the world with violence. But Noah prayed that the Lord would not let him ponder on such things during this time. He prayed for the ability to leave these things in the hands of his sovereign Creator and Lord. He reminded himself that in the big picture, the Lord was righteous and just.

He refocused his mind on the day's activities and looked out into the distance again. He thought surely that he could see a group of people heading this way! He smiled, thinking of how great it would be to see his father and grandfather again. It had been so many years since the last time they were together, times that all of them had come to cherish more and more.

Noah turned back toward the house and excitedly announced the approaching company. He could hear the movement inside from his wife scurrying about with last minute preparations. And soon she came out to stand beside him, and they strained their eyes to recognize specific faces as the wedding guests drew near.

Over the next few days, more and more guests arrived for the wedding celebration. Tents had been set up all across the hillside around Noah's home. Noah was cautious to verify that every person arriving truly belonged; he made sure they were all part of the family. Because there were a number of unfamiliar faces and names, he relied on those he knew to identify those he did not recognize. Noah had called a meeting of the family heads, and all agreed they would be responsible for the individuals in their group. Otherwise, Noah may have exhausted himself trying to keep an eye on the activities of so many guests.

Of course, the ark was a big attraction. And miraculously there were no accidents or damage done to the gigantic structure sitting in the valley below the house. Noah, Lamech, and Methuselah walked down to the ark the first day they arrived. Though Lamech was over 730 and Methuselah nearly 920 years old, they had no trouble maneuvering the slope to the site or walking around within the structure that was still under construction.

They carefully inspected the joints, the decking, the beams and rafters, studying the craftsmanship and sturdiness of all that Noah and his sons had completed. At each inspection point, they nodded their approval to one another, actually surprised at the quality of the work being done. They were both proud of Noah and his sons, for the skill of the work, but even more for allowing the LORD to accomplish this through them. Noah was very grateful to finally receive compliments for work well done rather than the typical taunts and ridicule he had received from those unwelcome visitors that frequented the area. When the tour had been completed, the men moved outside of the ark and paused there.

Noah's mind was wandering to thoughts of the future of his father and grandfather standing before him. He readily accepted the LORD's commands, but there were times that he wondered about some who would perish in the flood. He could see his father's lips moving; he was actually continuing with the compliments that had started during the tour. But Noah could not hear what he was saying. His mind was playing over the LORD's words: "Behold, I, even I am bringing the flood of water upon the earth, to destroy all flesh in which is the breath of life, from under heaven; everything that is on the earth shall perish. But I will establish my covenant with you; and you shall enter the ark—you and your sons and your wife, and your sons' wives with you." God had said you and your sons and your wife and your sons' wives with you. It couldn't be clearer to him. He felt guilty about questioning the LORD's judgment, but these men standing before him were more righteous than he was. They had not succumbed to the wicked influences of their time.

He was debating with himself, knowing that God was always right and just, but not understanding why he should go into the ark and not his father or grandfather. How could he explain these concerns to them? He began to pray for the LORD to give him the words, give him the answers he didn't have, give him the strength to know that God had not overlooked this detail.

He was just about to begin the mental debate about the wisdom of questioning God's plan and purpose when he felt hands grab his shoulders and shake him sternly. "Noah!"

His eyes were opened but not focused on anything until he felt the hands on his shoulders. Suddenly, he noticed his father's face was within a foot of his own. The eyes were piercing through his own, the voice calling his name again. "Noah!" Noah felt a little embarrassed as he realized his father was trying to bring him back to reality as his grandfather stood by with a concerned look on his face. They both realized he was back among them, and their worried faces relaxed. His father let go of one shoulder and moved to Noah's side, putting his other arm across his son's shoulders.

"Noah, your grandfather and I have talked at great length over the years about this ark. We have discussed it in particular on this journey regarding what we could say to you." Lamech's voice was soft but clear and deep. "Ever since you have told us about the LORD's plan for you and your family, we have realized the pressure that would be upon you. We never doubted that if the LORD called you, you would be capable of doing all he expected of you. God provides all things for those who will receive him." They were walking slowly around the ark, Lamech on the left with his arm around Noah and Methuselah on his right.

"We had no doubt about this." Methuselah motioned to the ark in a sweeping fashion. "But our concern has been how you would process the fact that we have not been included in the list of those to enter when the time is right. This must be a terrible burden for you, Noah." His grandfather put his hand on Noah's shoulder, and all three of them paused.

Methuselah looked into Noah's eyes now. Noah's eyes were filling up as the LORD spoke to him, "Listen to them, Noah," and he heard the voices of these men telling him that all would be well. A peace was coming over him as they continued, and his tears flowed. He didn't sob, but it felt very much like the day God had called him. He was overwhelmed. A burden was lifted as they began to walk again, and Noah was silent.

"Your father and I both have been visited by the Angel of the LORD, Noah. He has told us not to fear, that all would come to pass just as it had been explained to you. But we would not see that time." Noah stopped now and looked at Methuselah and then over at Lamech. He was very surprised. If they would not see the destruction of the world, then it could only mean one thing: the LORD would take them home before then.

"When?" he asked them both.

Lamech chuckled and they began walking once more. "He didn't share that with us, son. This is the very thing we have talked much about. We were never concerned for our welfare, for we know that God has assigned all of our days according to his purpose."

"We believe that we have been given this message to pass on to you. Surely, God had to know that this was weighing on your mind," Methuselah continued as if on cue. "He wants to have his faithful servant know that his God hears his prayers, knows his thoughts. We are to tell you that he will take care of us. You need not be troubled."

Lamech stepped in front of Noah and grabbed both of his shoulders again, and Methuselah moved beside Lamech. This time when they looked into his eyes, the eyes of both men were filling up also.

Lamech hugged Noah, holding him tight, whispering, "We are so very proud of you, my son. In the midst of all the violence and wickedness, you have been chosen as the Lord's servant."

He turned his face toward the heavens and hugged his son even tighter. "Thank you, God!" And the three of them stood there, eyes towards the heavens, each praying and praising and worshipping God, thanking him for the abundance of blessings they had been chosen to receive. And Noah prayed, giving a special thanks to God for easing his mind.

When they were done, Noah was smiling broadly, and his father and grandfather began to laugh. They walked around the ark again, this time Noah more animated, going over some of the details of construction the two old men may have overlooked. They made another tour inside and out, many times complimenting or commenting on the very things they had discussed the first time. But no one seemed to mind.

Hours later, when the sun was high in the sky, the men were almost to the top of the slope by the house. As was custom around Noah's home, they had all paused to look at the ark below as they silently admired all that had been done by the calling of God. Their thoughts were interrupted by the announcement of more guests arriving. And this time it was the grooms with their brides and the brides' families!

Noah slapped his father and grandfather on the shoulders and announced, "Let's go to a wedding, fellows!" They all laughed deep, roaring laughs as the three men hurried up the slope to see the approaching procession. Everyone was so excited and in the mood for a good time. Overhead, the angels that had visited Lamech and Methuselah watched over things, allowing nothing from the outside to approach this celebration ordained of God for the next several days.

The weddings were magnificent in everyone's mind. Nothing could have been done to make them better. There was more than enough food, wine, music, dancing, and conversation. Not one of the guests could ever recall a better time.

Each morning there was prayer and worship. Not everyone participated, but each day Noah, Lamech, and Methuselah prayed together in the morning and the evening. It was such a special time for them; they rarely had this opportunity due to the distances between them. Some of those who watched them as they prayed together would swear that they looked different when they arose after worship. Some said it was the spirit of God lighting their faces. Others thought it might have been other gods that had joined the wedding feast. But those other gods were never mentioned, nor did anyone dare to openly pray to those gods while they were on the land God had given Noah.

The wives Noah's sons had brought home were beautiful but very humble women. Immediately Noah's wife fell in love with each of them. They were very bright just as she was, Noah thought to himself, smiling.

On typical working days, Noah's wife was included in the prayer time with the men in the mornings and the evenings. But there were times during the day she could see from her vantage point Noah and her sons pausing from their work to collectively give praise to God. There were so many things to give God thanks for and pray over! She never needed company to pause and give thanks, but she found herself looking forward to the fellowship that she would now have with these young women throughout her day.

Just as Noah, Lamech, Methuselah, and Noah's sons spent time talking of things that men deal with, Noah's wife and the women spent much time together sharing the things the new brides would need to know. As it turned out, their parents had done well in raising these young women.

When the wedding feast had ended and all of the guests had returned to their homes, things returned to normal in the household of Noah and his expanding family. Other than Noah's discussions with his father and grandfather, not much had been spoken of concerning the ark. Of course, being the attraction it was, there had been many questions, and most of the guests had visited the site at one time or another. But whether it was spiritual intervention or just the distraction of the celebration, no one paid much attention to the explanations or the ark itself after the initial curiosities. But the time had come to make sure the new brides of Shem, Ham, and Japheth knew the significance of the ark.

The family had all gathered together to discuss exactly what they were doing each day, why they were doing it, and what was going to take place once it was completed. The young women listened intently, their eyes growing wide as the message that was given to Noah was explained to them. Noah talked for quite some time, and the ramifications of what the women were being told sank in as the evening wore on. Tears came into their eyes as they grasped what this meant to friends, family, and loved ones; it meant that they would all perish! It was so much to take in at one time, so they ended in prayer, asking for insight, understanding, and as always, gave praise to the living God as they worshipped him.

The very next day, Noah and his sons went back to work on the ark. Noah thought that perhaps his sons were working a little harder and seemed to be a little happier than he had recalled. They were more lighthearted and joked around with one another, and they always returned to work without any prodding or correction from their father. It appeared the boys were enjoying married life! They were good boys, and Noah was so very proud of them.

When the women came down together to bring the midday meal to the men, they stayed and had the meal together with the men. Noah and his wife sat beside one another and watched the interaction between the new couples. It was a wonderful thing to see, and it brought back memories of the early days in their own marriage. They smiled at one another, watching the love and the awkwardness between the three very different blossoming relationships. These would be long relationships together for these newlyweds. The future of the entire world was sitting before Noah and his wife. It was a sobering thought, but with God's guidance they had been able to give this new world the best start they knew how.

Noah and Ham looked up the ramp, their eyes slowly following the direction of the path up to the first level. Then, after pausing momentarily at the platform, their eyes followed the ramp as it took a turn in the direction of the ark, ending at the large solitary opening in the side of the massive structure. *Only one way in*, Noah thought. Once again, he had no idea in advance how this part of the project would turn out, but he had been guided every step of the way. It was his obedient heart that allowed him to receive the guidance, which he accepted willingly and without hesitation. The ramp ran parallel to the ark, upwards to a point about one half of the height to the opening that led to a large platform.

Then the ramp continued from the left side of the square platform up to the sole entrance. God's design had provided only one way into the ark, and this was the salvation offered by him. Upon close examination of the ramp, one could see that this second part of the ramp was hinged at the side of the ark and was actually the door that would seal up the ark once it was closed into place.

Noah and Ham looked at one another, both of them so proud of their work, and silently gave God thanks and praise for his guidance in the completion of this mammoth project. Ham slapped Noah on the shoulder and grinned broadly. He felt very good about all they were doing and trusted completely in his father's words that God had spoken to him about this. He also believed that God had given them all the skills and knowledge they needed to complete a productive day's work. His sons had never heard God speak. And since that day ninety-five years ago, Noah had not heard God's voice again. But none of them— Noah, his sons, his wife, or their wives—doubted for an instant that God was directing this work from beginning to end.

Shem appeared in the opening of the ark and called down to Noah and Ham at the base of the ramp. He motioned for them to come up. Noah bowed slightly and with a sweeping motion of his arm invited Ham to go first. Ham grinned as he started up the wide ramp with his father directly behind. It was a very sturdy walkway, gradually climbing to the first level. There was absolutely no give in the walkway as the two men went up. It could hold a lot more weight than the average man and never move or sway.

Ham met Shem and both turned to enter the ark together. Noah had slowed behind Ham so he could investigate the joints, the supports, the woodwork, and the hinged bottom as they climbed up into the great structure. He gave God thanks and praise again for the gifts he had given each of them to complete this wonderful and mysterious project. It still amazed Noah after all these years the way the LORD used him and his sons. As Noah entered the inside of the structure, he saw Ham and Shem following the ramps, moving up to the third level, no doubt to work on another task.

It was gratifying to Noah to see his sons take this work so seriously and without any hint of complaining. They seemed to enjoy the difficult work, the long hours, and at times, the unpleasant tasks that faced them each day. Noah then started down to the lower level.

Speaking of unpleasant tasks, Noah decided to check on Japheth, who was below applying pitch to the sides of the ark, inside and out, just as the LORD had commanded. By everyone's standards it was the most unpleasant task since they had started this project so many years ago. Fortunately for all of them, they shared the duty of applying pitch, as well as the other duties. This way no one was left to the least pleasant or the easiest jobs day in and day out.

Regardless of the tasks, the young men never grumbled or

complained, nor did they question the purpose of the work. It was not easy removing the sap that got on their hands or in their hair as they worked. So, whoever was applying the pitch would quit early to spend time cleaning up before dinner.

Noah found Japheth hard at work applying the seal to the walls of the ark. He did not hear his father coming or see Noah pause to smile when he heard Japheth humming softly as he worked. Noah could hear him softly verbalizing praise and worship to God as though he had reached the chorus in a song that he had composed as he went about the LORD's work. Noah thanked the LORD for such sons. Rather than going down and possibly disturbing the rhythm of his son's work and music, Noah turned to head back to the upper decks to find some new task of his own to get accomplished before the end of the day.

Strangers continued year after year to visit the site, coming to laugh at Noah and his family. They came to ridicule and to see for themselves if the stories they had heard were true. Some people went away changed by what they saw or heard. But they didn't stay changed. Not long after they were back in the elements that were prevalent throughout the world, they slipped back into the way of life they had known before. Most came to mock and left laughing. Nothing that was said to them would penetrate the veil of deception that had blinded them to the truth and to God.

But the work continued despite all the visitors. They had built all of the ark's body and now were putting on the roof and the openings that would let in the light, just as God had commanded. From atop the ark, it was easy to ignore the people below.

Since word of Lamech's death had come to them, Noah and his sons did not feel as though they had time to bother with the visitors. They were more sullen than they had ever been since the project had begun.

Noah's father had passed away quietly one evening in his sleep. Lamech's presence on this earth would surely be missed. He had followed God all of his days, just as Methuselah had raised him to do and just as he had passed on to Noah. It was becoming nearly impossible these days to find men who truly had a heart for God.

Noah explained to his family that it was okay to mourn the passing of Lamech for their own sake, but they should rejoice for his father was now with God. Noah smiled, picturing his father before God. But still his heart was heavy. He would miss him. Noah also explained to his family that he knew this was a sign that the day of the LORD was not far away. He had no idea of the day or the hour, but his father's passing was a sign that the time was drawing near. Noah knew that once his grandfather, Methuselah, passed away, the day to enter the ark would soon follow.

Although their spirits were heavy, Noah and his sons worked with a new intensity for the next few weeks. Slowly the pain of the loss eased, and things once again returned to normal. Japheth started humming and singing again when he thought no one was around to hear him. Shem, Ham, and Noah liked to listen to him, but they were very careful not to let him know they could hear him. They would often talk among themselves about Japheth's singing but never joked about it. They remarked about the feelings of peace and calm it gave them that they had not realized before.

As the next few years passed, many of the strangers that passed by saw that the ark was nearing completion and would ask more and more about the coming day. But these travelers were not seeking God's will or desiring to know his plan. Their intent was but to scoff and ridicule. They would ask Noah where his God was now that the boat was finished. Where was Noah's God who had prompted him to build this monstrosity so far from any body of water? It was an impressive structure, but it would be impossible to move to a source of water to see if it would even float!

They would ask him who had come up with this shape and size. It was nothing like the boats and vessels that anyone had ever seen. Some even tried to convince him that converting this into a temple would be a great idea, that they could become rich! The story of the crazy man in the wilderness was known far and wide. People would come and worship at this "temple." What they were worshipping, Noah didn't want to imagine.

Noah no longer took time for these people; so many had come and gone. Often they would return with their friends, as if this were a tourist attraction. But the Lord had revealed to Noah that everyone who came was beyond help at this point. He, along with Shem, Ham, and Japheth, just ignored them and continued with their work.

This irritated the most unbearable of the scoffers. After all, they had brought friends to hear the rantings of Noah, whom they referred to with disdain as the "holy man." It was all a big joke, a big farce, and a big mistake. And when they went away, those who had brought them out would tell the newcomers of the wild stories they used to hear from Noah about the destruction of the earth and all mankind. And they continued on, marrying, buying, selling, and trading as if all was right with the world.

> My Spirit will not contend with man forever, for he is mortal; his days will be a hundred and twenty years.
>
> Genesis 6:3

THE FINAL GATHERING

> You are to bring into the ark two of all living creatures, male and female, to keep them alive with you. Two of every kind of bird, of every kind of animal and of every kind of creature that moves along the ground will come to you to be kept alive.
>
> Genesis 6:19

The dew seemed to hang on the grass longer than usual this particular morning. A young doe was grazing peacefully as the sun climbed higher in the sky, warming her back and eliminating all traces within her of the previous evening's chill. There was no sense of alarm in the air, just a peace that hung over this high mountain meadow. All around her other does and bucks grazed. There was no sense of urgency, no sense of danger.

Suddenly, she raised her head with a start. Her large ears went straight up. They were open and alert for any sound. She surveyed the surrounding terrain for any signs of danger. But no other member of the herd had raised its head from its morning meal. She was not afraid, though her large white tail twitched repeatedly. There was nothing there, nothing out of the ordinary. But she did not go back to her grazing. She stood perfectly still, her ears twisting slowly back and forth as she stared down toward the valley below.

God gently placed his hand on her back, and immediately she felt a complete calm and peace come over her, something she could feel but could not understand. She began to move slowly as though she was headed for a better patch of the sweet mountain grass.

The LORD turned his head toward the herd they were slowly leaving behind. Immediately a young buck's head shot up. He was tall and strong, with a new set of seasonal antlers just coming in. He saw the young doe heading down the meadow away from the rest of the herd. Without really knowing why, he followed. He paced his gait a little quicker than the doe until they were side by side. He looked down at her, and she turned her head toward him. They looked at one another as if each expected some sort of answer or explanation. But there was only silence. They just knew they had somewhere to go.

The LORD walked with them, his hands resting gently on the back of each, but only for a short distance. And he was gone; the two deer had never actually seen him. From the farthest corners of the earth similar scenes were taking place, going totally unnoticed by the world around them; pairs of animals were starting off on a journey with no idea where it would take them.

On this same morning, Noah finished his prayers and started to make his way down the hill to the ark, which rested quietly below. As he had done each morning over these many years, he paused to survey the site from above. From this vantage point he could easily take in the entire structure. But this morning he paused longer than usual.

Shem, Ham, and Japheth, having finished their prayers, came up behind their father. As had become their custom, they too looked down over the site. Shem spoke first, breaking the silence. "What shall we do today?"

They all stood waiting for the response from Noah, who continued to stare down over the ark below. Shem looked over at Ham when Noah did not respond to his question. Ham looked back at his brother and shrugged his shoulders. He then looked over at Japheth to see if he might have some idea of what their father might be thinking. It was obvious Japheth did not have any answers either, as he simply raised his eyebrows in response to their stares.

After a very long pause, Noah turned toward his sons. He looked at them as though he had just come out of some sort of trance. With his back to the ark, Noah announced to his sons very matter-of-factly, "We won't go down to the ark today. It's time for the harvest; it's time to gather some food."

Noah walked toward his sons, and they parted to allow him to pass. He headed toward the house and the fields beyond. His sons looked at one another, then down again at the ark, then back to one another. Shem thought of encouraging his father to have at least one of them go down to work on the ark. After all, the harvest was not due for at least two more weeks. Though, he admitted there might be some crops ready to yield now. He thought if he suggested a specific task, his father would agree that it made perfect sense to have someone continue the work they had been doing nearly all one hundred years since their birth!

But as he thought about what tasks needed to be completed, he could not come up with a thing left undone. As this realization began to sink in, he looked at his brothers and said, "It's time for the harvest." He walked past Ham and Japheth and followed in his father's footsteps.

Ham looked at Japheth and Japheth watched as Ham proceeded after Shem. Japheth took another look down at the ark and thought to himself that it would feel odd not to make the trip down as they had done every other day. He shrugged his shoulders and followed the rest of the men to the fields.

> You are to take every kind of food that is to be eaten and store it away as food for you and for them.
>
> Genesis 6:21

So Noah and his sons gathered their harvest. They collected fruits and vegetables, stored some, prepared the remainder, and stored them away as well. The entire family worked each day from sunrise to sunset. They kept a diligent, steady, and focused pace so that all tasks were carried out. The women stored, packed, and dried figs, dates, flour, grains, and meals. At the same time, the men gathered the crops and made them ready for storage. As they were storing their goods into the ark, they began to understand God's reasoning for the unusual design of this enormous vessel; it contained an abundance of storage space! There seemed to be no end to the room that had been set aside for the storage of the food and supplies.

It was during this time that word came of Methuselah's passing. Like Lamech just about five years before, he had passed away quietly in his sleep. There was no time for mourning. Noah knew and assured his family that this was just as God had planned. They need not worry about leaving their loved ones behind when the flood came.

Since the ark had been started, righteous family members and loved ones had passed away, as was God's plan. Yes, there were other family members that were still living among them all. But they had chosen their paths long ago. Those that Noah and his wife knew to be godly people, who were sincerely following God's ways, were with them now and would enter the ark. Noah thought back to the time during his sons' weddings when both Lamech and Methuselah had told him not to fear for them. God surely took care of his children.

When Noah and his family had completed gathering all the crops and fruits to be harvested, he recalled God's words, "…food for you and for them." Then Noah collected every type of hay, straw, nut, seed, flower, and the things that would sustain the creatures that God had told him would enter. And then there were unusual things they collected, though they were not sure why. But it was revealed to them by their God to gather these things and store them away. This process continued for months as they continued to follow their God's mysterious plan.

One sunny afternoon, Japheth and his wife went into the forest just a short way from the house and the ark to gather cones, green twigs, and leaves. They were filling a basket that would go over Japheth's head and rest on his back; it was much easier to balance and carry a large quantity that way. Japheth was working and gathering the things they needed that were in abundance here. He was thinking to himself, as many times as he had been in these woods, he had never paused to notice the rich fertile land and foods God had provided for all the animals that he had created.

He looked over to speak to his wife, who had been gathering berries nearby, but then he noticed she had stopped working. She stood staring in his direction, her eyes wider than he had ever seen them, and her mouth was open as if in shock. He started to move toward her to see what the problem was, but as he let go of his basket, her hand raised slowly, her mouth still agape, and pointed at him, or was it past him to something beyond? He was concerned for her and found it difficult to look away. But as her arm raised and her eyes grew wider, he made himself slowly turn to the direction she was pointing behind where he stood.

Now it was Japheth's turn to stand frozen with his eyes wide and his mouth dropped open. As he stared in disbelief, he backed slowly toward his wife until he was by her side. He reached down and held her hand in his. He never took his eyes off the spectacle before them.

No more than forty cubits away, slowly and methodically moving through the trees, a behemoth had paused to grab a mouthful of leaves and small green twigs high above the ground. It paused for a moment to chew and then turned its head away from the two stunned humans to look at another of its kind passing by just a short distance farther into the trees. The first creature that was still chewing its food continued on its way, never even noticing Japheth and his wife who were watching in silent awe.

Its head was hidden in the tops of the trees, and its enormous feet that were attached to legs as big as cedars were holding up a body that was massive! The tail was the size of a tree, yet it moved with a kind of grace. Surprisingly, there were no powerful thuds or ground shaking as those enormous feet hit the ground. They could hear them walking, but Japheth nor his wife had heard them approaching.

Once the enormous creatures had moved out of sight, Japheth and his wife gathered their things and ran back to the ark as fast as their feet would take them. Noah and the rest of the family had been bringing provisions into the ark to store. When Japheth and his wife exited the forest, they noticed the behemoths had come out also; the creatures were far off to their left, out in the meadow. Japheth thought this was amazing since they could actually show the others what they had seen.

As they ran toward the ark, Japheth realized he had no fear of these creatures, just fascination and an appreciation of God's creation. He saw his father standing in the doorway of the ark, and he began calling and waving his arms to get his attention while they were still a long way off. Noah waved back at them, though he seemed distracted, not really paying much attention. By the time they had reached the ramp leading into the ark, Shem and his wife had joined Noah at the entrance. They too did not seem focused on the couple running to speak to them.

When Japheth and his wife had run up the ramp to the platform level and turned to go up the last leg, they both stopped running, realizing they were nearly out of breath. Noah smiled down at them as they neared him. Japheth grinned broadly, anxious to speak to his father. "Father!" he gasped, trying to catch his breath. "You won't—" he stopped in midsentence as Noah pointed back over Japheth's shoulder toward the open countryside beyond. Japheth and his wife moved up to Noah, Shem, and his wife and turned to look in the direction his father was pointing.

"They're coming," Noah said. Out across the rolling expanse of the valley, there were animals of every type moving in the general direction of the ark.

"Two of every kind of bird, or every kind of animal and of every kind of creature that moves along the ground will come to you to be kept alive." Noah recalled the words the LORD had spoken to him one hundred years before. And now it was coming to pass. For the moment, Japheth and his wife forgot about their encounter in the forest just a short time ago. There were lions walking among the deer, foxes with the squirrels, and wolves with rabbits!

They were neither prey nor victim, but all were traveling companions who appeared to have established a truce among them. Some of them continued past the ark into the meadows beyond, and some wandered into the forests seeking shade, a place to rest or feed. And they all moved in pairs—two foxes, two bears, and two giraffes; two by two they moved toward the ark.

They were coming from as far as Noah and his family watching in wonder could see, and many had moved past. For the most part, they ignored the humans and the ark. Apparently it was not yet time for them to enter. It seemed as though there was an endless stream of beasts that moved on the ground and creatures that flew through the air. Some creatures were of great beauty and grace while others were hideous and fearful. But every one of them was a part of God's creation.

From atop the hill near their home, Noah's wife, along with Ham and his wife, had ceased their chores and were looking down over the valley at the approach of the creatures. They were huddled in a tight group, hugging one another and smiling so much it was hurting their faces. They had never doubted Noah's calling from God, and they knew that the fact the ark stood completed below was confirmation. But this gathering they were witnessing was an unparalleled spectacle on its own. It had overwhelmed them with God's graciousness, his mercy, his power, and his presence. They were so overcome they found it hard to breathe.

As the procession of creatures continued to gather, they saw flamingos, peacocks, eagles, and great numbers of other bird species too numerous to mention. They were all flying over the gathering places, seeking a place to land and rest from their journey. Ham, his wife, and his mother made their way down to the ark and up the ramp to join the rest of their family. And now every creature to be saved from the day of the LORD had gathered in this one place.

All the members continued to gather food with a new and exciting outlook. As they moved among the creatures and noted different food items that were being consumed, they made a point to stock up on that favored food item. The gathering process went on, and the creatures great and small just lingered close to the ark moving about but never straying far. They were waiting for something, as if they knew it would not be long now. And the humans gathering the food felt the same sense— not long now.

ONLY ONE WAY
TO SALVATION

The LORD then said to Noah, "Go into the ark, you
and your whole family, because I have found you
righteous in this generation."

Genesis 7:1

It was early morning, and the sun had chased away the chilly
autumn darkness. But it had not yet climbed over the distant
mountains, revealing its brilliant rays of promise for a new day.
Noah had just started up the ramp to enter the ark. It was easy
to see all around him, and at any moment he would see the
piercing rays of God's creation. His light would ease over the
top of the horizon. It would shoot its welcoming rays across the
floor of the valley, bringing the warmth and comfort of a sunny
November morning as only God could provide.

Noah paused for a moment as he noticed something out of
the corner of his eye. There, at the base of the ramp, no more
than two cubits from the bottom, he saw a snail—no, wait—two
snails making their way along the outer edge of the entry ramp.

Noah grinned, wondering if they had received some insight from God or perhaps were getting ahead of themselves here.

He turned his gaze up the ramp and tried to imagine from their perspective the long journey ahead. Then, for just a moment, he wondered how far these two had already traveled to get to this point. He turned to look back over his shoulder, across the valley filled with animals of all kinds. They were beginning to stir and rise up just as he and his family had to greet a new day.

"Noah!" Noah recognized that voice. It had been one hundred years since he had last heard it, but he knew without a doubt who was calling his name. Noah dropped to his knees and fell to his face in reverence to his sovereign Creator.

"Go into the ark, you and your whole family, because I have found you righteous in this generation." Noah, with his face to the walkway that led to salvation, did not move, but received all that the Lord had said. At this moment he was totally focused on the significance of the message: "Go into the ark." The Lord's obedient servant listened with his whole being.

"Take with you seven of every kind of clean animal, a male and its mate, and two of every kind of unclean animal, a male and its mate, and also seven of every kind of bird, male and female, to keep their various kinds alive throughout the earth. Seven days from now I will send rain on the earth for forty days and forty nights, and I will wipe from the face of the earth every living creature I have made."

Noah remained prostrate, hearing the words of God over and over. Either he wasn't sure if there was more to come or he was, as he had been one hundred years ago, so totally overwhelmed by the fact that God had spoken to him that he could not move. He had faithfully built the ark on the very word of God. He and his sons diligently worked for a century to complete this monumental task. When the ark was completed, they had stored food for the animals and themselves, just as God had commanded. Everything seemed to be complete. But Noah never considered going in until the time was right. And until now, God had not revealed to him what would be the right time to enter.

He lifted himself to a kneeling position, turned his head toward heaven, and prayed aloud. He praised God and thanked him for the continual provision and for seeing his humble servant as being worthy to speak to. Noah knew that he could never fully understand the ways or the mind of the Creator of all things.

As he continued praying, his family gathered behind him. They did not hear anything God said to Noah, but they knew that he was receiving final instructions. They looked at one another, each in turn, their eyes revealing the understanding that it was time. After one hundred years it was time for the final instructions and preparation for the day of the LORD!

They would not interrupt Noah's prayers, and after a short time looking back and forth to one another, Noah's wife, Shem, Ham, Japheth, and their wives all dropped down to their knees to pray. They held hands together in a tight circle, praying silently whatever was in their heart, lifting it up in prayer to their sovereign God.

When Noah rose, the prayer circle behind him ended and they rose as well. As the servant-leader of the group that God had chosen rose to his feet, the family waited for him to speak. His back was still to them, and he looked ahead to the opening in the ark for a long moment as he pondered on that opening, that single, solitary way that led to salvation. He thought of those in the world, many that had come here discounting what he had to say to them. They believed they were just fine. They had made sacrifices to their gods. They had not really hurt many people, and they thought they were living good lives. They knew they did not deserve to die, and so this crazy man's story was just that, a story!

Noah looked at the only way in. His story had not been remembered by them. They would go on living as they always had. He finally turned back to see his family waiting a short distance from where he stood. He glimpsed quickly down and saw the snails making their way steadily up the ramp. *It had to start somewhere*, he thought.

"We should gather our things from the house. Take clothing, bowls, utensils, our entire household. We should bring them down. The LORD has told me that in just seven days the waters will come and wipe out everything that he had created. In seven days…" Noah's voice trailed off. What else could he say? He explained to them about bringing the clean animals in groups of seven and the birds into the ark.

When he had told them all that the LORD had revealed, the sons rushed off towards the house to begin gathering the sheep, oxen, and goats that they had raised. The women followed and began gathering the household things they thought they would need, doing their best to be selective.

Noah watched them move off and then looked out over the incredible variety of animals before him. He quietly raised his eyes to his God and began to pray. "LORD God, Heavenly Father, Creator of all, Sovereign Ruler," Noah closed his eyes and completed his prayer, "this should be very interesting." He bowed his head and gave God thanks and praise, knowing full well, as interesting as it may be, the LORD would provide the way to make it all happen. He would provide the way just as he provided the salvation for him and his precious family.

When all of their supplies had been stored away, the family again stopped and looked at each other. They were on the third level in an area that had been set aside for them, and all things had been put away in preparation for the time to come. They all paused, and the look on each face asked the same question, "What now?"

Noah took the lead and without speaking moved to the second level and out to the entrance. As he stepped out onto the entryway, he stopped. The family moved in behind and around him, stopping at the entrance also. There at the bottom of the ramp stood a young doe, watching the people at the top as she bent her head low to sniff the ramp. To her right stood a large young buck, watching the group above intently. His ears pitched forward, his nostrils flaring, sniffing the air for any sign of danger. Sensing none, he began to move, putting one hoof on the boards, then another, and slowly, cautiously started up the ramp. Before he had put his last back hoof on the boards, the doe followed right behind.

From above, Noah felt his heart began to beat high in his chest as if it were trying to get out through his throat. He felt God's presence everywhere. The women had tears in their eyes as they watched the scene unfolding before them. The men did not cry, but it was only by the greatest of restraints that they did not. The scene of these two young deer coming up on their own for the salvation they had chosen to accept was almost too much to contain.

Behind them, a pair of horses moved in, tossing their manes in the air, snorting excitedly and shaking their heads. They could feel God's presence too. And all across the valley, as if in unison, the masses of animals began to move towards the ark; one pair after another was moving into place behind the next pair to move forward. It was an awe-inspiring sight to see the animals going into the ark towards Noah and his family. They were coming two by two, just as God had commanded.

There were some pens or corralled areas inside that were larger than others. And just as with most of the construction process, Noah had no idea what animals should go where. But the LORD was orchestrating this ballet. As the animals began to enter, Shem, Ham, and Japheth followed them in. They didn't have to lead; they just watched as the creatures seemed to know exactly where to go, whether the lower deck, the middle deck, or the upper deck. The largest of the animals were drawn below, and it soon became clear that the design inside was just as it needed to be to accommodate all who were accepting this grace and mercy from the LORD.

The women moved inside, went above, and watched from a vantage point on the third level. Noah stayed at the door. He felt that the LORD would have him stand there as the beacon. He would be the familiar landmark the creatures were to seek so they would know they were in the right place.

God had sent them to Noah. Standing there alone, Noah could not contain the tears any longer. God had filled his heart this day. For Noah to actually see what he was seeing and experience what he was experiencing was too much for him to keep inside. He kept raising his head to the heavens giving silent, heartfelt thanks and praise to God. And the Angel of the Lord, who stood at Noah's side, was smiling.

Inside, Shem, Ham, and Japheth were walking in a sort of daze among the animals that entered. They could hardly believe what was going on, and they were doing nothing other than observing. The animals were doing just as God had commanded.

The parade continued day after day, moving slowly but deliberately. To their surprise, there was no rush or anxiousness among the animals that time was running out. As God had said, it would be seven days.

THE DAY OF THE LORD

And I will wipe from the face of the earth every living creature I have made.

Genesis 7:4

It was business as usual in the village this particular day. People were hurrying to their destinations; they were eating, drinking, and carrying on business just like they had always done. Those selling idols to the people were counting their profits. Those who served at the high places were doing the same, counting their profits. This day was no different than the day that Noah had experienced 120 years earlier on his journey into the village—only much closer to destruction than before.

The man Noah had rescued was still with the woman who had taken him in. They had figured a way to join forces and combine talents. They were quite effective at taking advantage of people. The Nephilim had congregated here, just as they had done in many other places when they found they could use the stories and tales of old to gain advantage. Then they abused the misguided trust and faith the people had placed in them. But their numbers were great and no one would oppose them. They did whatever pleased them, whenever it pleased them. And everyone in their community accepted it.

Business was as usual, so much so that no one noticed beyond a casual glance that the sky grew dark and the clouds were gathering. A cool, autumn breeze picked up and grew in intensity. Soon after, many started to pull their cloaks or shawls tightly around their necks and heads in an attempt to ward off the chilly wind. They were covering their faces from the flying dirt and sand as the wind grew stronger.

The winds seemed to be gathering the clouds. They were black and ominous in appearance. They blew in over the village, covering the entire sky. What they did not see was that beyond the village the clouds were gathering over the entire earth. When the wind started to die down, the pace of the village slowed with it. All the people suddenly noticed the darkening sky. The black clouds had blotted out the sun to the point that it appeared as if evening had suddenly come upon them. No one quite knew what to make of this.

The priests, idol makers, and sellers ignored their concerns about what was going on around them and began to formulate plans to profit from the situation. They would convince the people that one or more of the gods were angry. Perhaps they needed another idol because they were worshipping the wrong deity. This could make for really big takings.

Then without warning, in an instant, a great rift in the ground opened up in the middle of the village square. It started in the center and ran out in two directions from east to west. As the divide lengthened, the center grew wider and wider. Rocks and earth crumbled into the growing chasm. The ground was trembling like an earthquake that grew in intensity. People could not get out of the way quick enough, and the growing abyss swallowed scores of them up.

The people were running and screaming, not sure where to go, but trying to get as far away from danger as was humanly possible. Some fell prostrate and began to pray, leaving their life in the hands of the broken idols laying in pieces on the ground where they had fallen, either knocked over from the tremors or trampled by the fleeing masses.

Buildings began to crumble as the tremors grew louder. Then the waters came. It looked like a huge geyser as the fountains of the deep burst out of the ground with an explosion and rose into the air high above the village. When it reached its highest point, the fountain mushroomed out away from the center at its peak, and the waters came back to the earth. The volume was so great that in just moments the square was covered in water and was rising quickly.

Those who had thrown themselves to the ground begging for salvation from their lifeless gods were suddenly hit with the realization that they were all alone. Their idols were smashed in pieces on the ground and were now submerged. The gods they had chosen to trust and worship could do nothing to help them.

The great fountain grew wider and longer, coming out of the chasm with a force that no man had ever seen before nor would ever see again. There was so much panic and terror that the people did not notice the floodgates of the sky had opened up and let loose blankets of water that joined with the fountains of the deep. God had released all the waters that had been gathered from the beginning of time above the land and in the deep below the land. There was nowhere to run except into the upper levels of the village buildings.

Those who were not in the immediate center of the village where the fountains burst forth had tried to run from the village as though this was a localized punishment to this community alone. But out in the open, they were now being slowed to a crawl as the water rose to knee deep, then soon, waist deep.

From the upper rooms, those who had managed to escape from the streets looked out away from the village in horror. They watched the sky rip open, the waters pouring out, and more fountains that had burst forth from other rifts in the earth as far as they could see. A sense of the impending doom fell over most in the upper rooms. They grew quiet, and more than one of them thought of a crazy man in the wilderness pleading with them to change, to hear the warnings and turn to his God.

Some figured he was busy treading water or looking for higher ground just as they were. Some knew better. And yet, they still would not turn to the one true God the crazy man had preached for them to accept, to acknowledge, to worship, and to put their faith in. They were safe from the water for now. But they could not ignore the rate at which the floodwaters rose.

They watched out over the landscape, watching as many who had tried to flee were being overcome by the waters and the waves; they grew stronger and higher as the waters from above falling to the earth collided with the waters from below reaching up to the heavens. They watched as the currents and waves began to crumble the buildings around them, tearing them to pieces. They were protected in their sanctuary by the surrounding buildings that were taking the brunt of the force from the water. But as those buildings crumbled to pieces and disappeared into the sea rising all around, they knew their time was very short.

Noah and his family entered the ark. It had been seven days, and Noah had done everything according to all the Lord had commanded. He paused at the doorway as the last of his family members entered through the only way in. Back across the valley that just a few days earlier had been covered with animals of every kind, the water was flowing in and rising fast. All around in the distance he could see fountains of water climbing high into the sky. There had been no splits in the earth immediately around the ark's resting place, but they had felt the ground tremble just a short time ago. The day of the Lord had begun. They had seen the dark clouds gather and the day grew dark and ominous.

Noah was 600 years old, and it was the second month, the seventeenth day in the month of November. At the Lord's command, he had been preparing for this day for one hundred years. And now God would blot out every living thing on the face of the earth with the exception of those creatures behind him in the ark.

As he turned to enter, the floodgates of the sky opened up and the rains began. Noah turned back around and listened to this strange new sound of water falling from the sky. He watched the intensity at which the water fell, and as it did, the floodwaters rose. As he stood there watching, his family came to stand around him, silently observing the spectacle. And as they stood there, the door of the ark began to rise up. It separated from the end of the ramp and slowly began to close. They all just stood there watching in amazement as it closed tightly into place. From the outside, God sealed his chosen inside, the only way to salvation that he had provided.

> For forty days the flood kept coming on the earth, and as the waters increased they lifted the ark high above the earth. The waters rose and increased greatly on the earth, and the ark floated on the surface of the water.

> Genesis 7:17–18

They all stood in the dimly lit entryway holding hands together while Noah led them in prayer. Before they had finished, they began to hear the ark creak and groan. At first it was almost too quiet to be heard, and then it would stop. But as the rain continued to pound relentlessly on the roof of the ark, the creaking grew more frequent and became louder.

The family finished their prayers and was on their way to the third level when they felt the first movement. Just as the creaking had first begun, the first movement was so slight that they were not sure if they had really felt it. But soon there was no doubt that the huge vessel was lifting off its foundations where it had rested these past one hundred years.

There was a tilting on one side, though very slight, and then the other side would tilt and straighten the ark again. Before long, though they could not see exactly what was going on outside, they felt the unmistakable rocking of the ark on the waves. What they could not see were the size of the waves and churning waters that it took to rock the enormous vessel. Two-thirds of the ark rode above the waters while one-third (about eleven cubits) sat below the surface.

All across the world, the fountains of the deep had burst open, and the canopies of the heavens had been laid open at the same time. The forces of the water were so great that anyone who tried to climb to the heights above the rising body of water was washed off the sides of the mountains. Those who had made it to the lower mesas and ridges had just a short time before the waters overcame their positions.

In the coastal areas, many were fortunate enough, or so they thought, to make it to the ships and vessels that traveled the seas and fresh bodies of water. But these crafts could not stand against the tidal waves and the boiling, churning waters that tossed these ships about. The fountains that had burst forth from the depths of the earth were now submerged but still sending forth torrents of water. They were no longer rising high into the air like geysers because of the depth of the flood over them, but there was such force behind them the areas on the surface boiled like a gigantic heated cauldron. Ships and boats that chanced to be driven too near were overcome by the violent action of the floodwaters. Those ships that did not get trapped in the turbulent waters were no match for the torrents pouring from the heavens. There had never been rains such as these before or since this terrible day of the LORD. If one can imagine the worst of hurricanes, monsoons, or typhoons, all pale in comparison to these days. Nothing was spared outside of the ark.

Back inside the ark, Noah and his family were spared the screams of terror from those perishing outside. They could not see but could hear the pouring curtains of rain and the churning fountains of the deep that pounded the top and the sides of the great ark. The relentless sounds drowned out any other from the outside.

The waters rose so fast that even those who thought of the crazy man in the wilderness and longed to have another opportunity to hear his message never had a last chance to make the short journey to salvation. All were overcome in the same places they had lived and spent their lives rejecting God. They had chosen their way of life, and now they had chosen their eternity.

Noah and his family settled in for their journey, not having any idea how long they would be inside the ark. They prepared a meal and settled into the quarters they had set up for themselves. The animals were unusually calm, undisturbed by the noise and activity outside. Noah imagined they were giving thanks for being among the chosen just as his family had been.

As the waters grew deeper and deeper, the ark rose, floating over the surface, driven by the winds and currents. There was no way to steer the vessel, so Noah never concerned himself with avoiding obstacles or setting direction. God was the captain of this ship of salvation. He would provide the direction and the destination just as he had for Noah all of his life, just as he had for all of the other people of the earth for their whole lives. The only difference was that Noah had faith and chose to listen, trusting in the direction God would lead.

Day after day the rains poured endlessly from the heavens. For "forty days and forty nights," the LORD had told Noah. The fountains of the deep continued to release the waters from below as well. But the more the waters rose, the less turbulence from the fountains was evident at the surface. But there was no one to see the difference.

Noah and his family could not see through the driving rain even if they did choose to go to the openings that would allow light in. And there was not one living being left outside to witness. All flesh and all mankind in whose nostrils was the breath of the spirit of life died. The waters rose over the highest mountains under heaven until they were covered by at least fifteen cubits (more than twenty-two feet) of the floodwater.

Each day, though it was hard to tell the evenings from the daytime during the deluge, Noah rose and started with his morning prayers, giving thanks to God. Most days, his family rose with him and joined in the morning praise before starting their day. But some days Noah woke before the others. And when he had spent his time with God and was feeling refreshed and at peace, he would wander around the levels of the ark.

Many of the animals were still asleep, and he did his best not to disturb them. Some of the birds had built nests in the corners up among the rafters. The owls would watch him intently when he quietly walked through on these mornings. Noah would watch in awe as the birds would follow his every move, only turning their heads, until it looked like their heads were sitting backwards on their bodies.

The animals in the ark were a miracle of the Creator, and Noah would watch in fascination the uniqueness of each of them. Some that he found to be awake would come to the edge of their pens or corrals to see Noah when he made these daily visits. The horses and the deer in particular loved to have him rub behind their ears and stroke their foreheads and muzzles.

Some of the animals seemed to sleep all the time, as though they were in hibernation. Noah could not recall seeing some of them awake since they had come into the ark. He would watch them closely and observe the steady rise and fall of their backs or sides, knowing they were alive and breathing. He had concluded this was a part of the Lord's plan also. Noah knew that God had allowed him to be a part of the construction and the preparations. But he also had a sense that there were a great many things that had gone on, and were going on, that he had no part in at all.

God had gathered two of every animal from the earth; he had brought them to Noah and aboard the ark. He had given Noah exactly what he needed to build the ark, and he himself had sealed up the ark behind Noah and his family just as the rains and floods began. Noah would seriously wonder at times what unseen things had been going on these past one hundred years in God's plan for all of this.

> ... I will send rain on the earth for forty days and forty nights ...
>
> Genesis 7:4

The constant drumming of the rain had become such a part of everyone's day that all had ceased to pay any attention to it. So it was on this particular day as Shem was on the second level putting more feed out for the animals. Each day he, Ham, and Japheth would make sure the animals were fed and had plenty of drinking water. The winds that came in through the openings above kept the ark from getting too warm. With all of the body heat from the animals, especially at the lower levels, it could have become very oppressive and uncomfortable. The way the LORD had designed the roof and the openings, the water would not get in, but the winds could enter and kept the air circulating throughout the vessel. It was dark more often than not because the clouds did not allow much light to enter. So, often lamps had to be carried as they went to the lower decks.

As Shem was putting some hay in with the horses and reaching into the manger where he would drop the hay, he stopped and paused midway and turned his head and listened closely. Ham was just coming up from the lower levels. He started to engage in conversation with his brother, reporting on something that was going on below, when he was shushed. Ham was a little upset and started to object. "What do you mean by shushing me?"

"SSSHHH!" Shem insisted and tilted his head a little more as if it would help him hear more clearly. Ham, sensing this was serious, walked quietly up to his brother, who dropped the hay into the manger and stopped. He tried to listen too. He even tilted his head, but in the opposite direction.

Finally he gave up and straightened up. "I don't hear anything. What do you hear?" he asked his brother.

Shem grabbed his shoulders and looked into his eyes and broke into a large grin. "I don't hear anything either!"

Ham looked at his brother and wondered if the darkness and the routine were starting to get to Shem. Then he thought perhaps it was the pounding of never-ceasing rain from ... Ham's eyes grew very large. He began to grin also. "I don't hear anything either!"

The two brothers hugged one another and stood there laughing. They turned together and ran up to the top deck. They started to call for their father and mother but realized that they did not have to announce anything. The rest of the family was looking to the openings where a different kind of light, one not filtered through sheets of rain and black clouds, filtered in.

Noah looked back at his sons and put out one arm and invited them to come over. His other arm was around his own wife's waist as he held her close. As Ham and Shem joined them, they could see their mother weeping tears of joy, and then they noticed their own wives straining to fight back tears of joy; they were quickly at their husbands' sides. Everyone stood there for a long while, smelling the fresh air, soaking up the light, and enjoying the sound of no rain. After forty days, just as God had told them, the rains ceased. And it was the third month, on the twenty-seventh day.

> The waters flooded the earth for a hundred and fifty days.
>
> Genesis 7:24

The ark drifted on the surface of the waters, being driven by the direction of the winds, the currents of the deep, the hand of God. The passengers inside had no clue where they were headed or how far from home they were. Not that it mattered of course, for there was no longer home as they once knew it. There was no destination at this time. All of the potential destinations were submerged.

In the days following the ceasing of the rains, Noah would open the windows above to let the light and the breezes in. He would look out over the vast expanse of water for any sign of land. But other than God's canvas in the sky, which seemed to be a new masterpiece each day, there was no landmark.

When the rain stopped, there was an excitement and a new hope of things to come. The solemn tone that had existed during the seemingly never-ending rains was replaced with a new energy from the caretakers on board. They all kept busy throughout the day caring for the needs of the animals and themselves. There was much less work for the men, who had no need to gather food or spend time working on the construction of the ark.

And so, it was the men who first began to feel restless. Noah never faltered in his faith that the Lord had a plan from the beginning to the end. And by that, he knew it included the building of the ark to the starting a whole new world. He knew in his heart that God had planned each detail of every day for every human he created. And he never doubted.

But Ham began to wonder when and if they would ever be out of the ark. He tried to keep it to himself, but as the days turned into weeks, and the weeks into months, his attitude and behavior changed noticeably. Sometimes he would retreat from the family without saying a word. Sometimes he would snap at his brothers if they tried to joke around with him. Everyone was praying for the day they could leave the ark, but it just seemed to affect Ham more than the others.

Ham felt very grateful that he had his wife. He felt he could talk with her when they were alone and he could release his building frustration from being cooped up for so long. She tried to understand and would occasionally share her suggestive assistance but learned that it was better to listen and be there for him rather than try to fix the situation or explain why he needed to have more faith.

Noah noticed his son's gloomy mood and thought he should try to speak with him. But that did not affect Ham's dark mood. Noah was living in faith that God had a better day prepared for them. But the Lord had not revealed to Noah how long they would be in the ark. So he could not tell Ham anything certain.

Noah told him that the Lord would not keep them inside any longer than was necessary and Noah knew that it would not be more than they could handle. But that was too uncertain for Ham; it offered him no consolation. Noah tried to help Ham remember the works of the Lord that he had witnessed: the building of the ark, the gathering of the animals, the rains, and the flood. Those things came about just as God had promised. And God had promised a covenant with them. Ham knew his father was right, but he felt so closed in, even in the expanse of the ark. He longed to touch the ground again, to wander the forests, to work the ground! He tried to be more social, but before long his sullen mood crept back in and he just wanted to be alone.

Noah prayed for his son, that God would help him cope better. The others noticed too, and they did what they could to bring Ham out of his depression. It worked to some extent. Ham could see everyone trying so hard to help, so he made an extra effort to not snap at them or to not be too negative. But his mind often wandered to things in the past.

Shem and Japheth also struggled at times with the feeling of being cooped up. But they handled it differently than Ham. Perhaps it was seeing Ham so affected by it that these two would not let it get the best of them. They often turned to God and prayed for perseverance, and most times turning to their Creator was enough. But some days seemed more difficult than others. So they would speak to their wives, to their father, to one another. And without fail, they would find the comfort and fellowship they needed.

The women seemed to have plenty to do with keeping the clothes clean, preparing meals, and picking up after the men. And they talked with one another about their struggles, their husbands' struggles, and all the things that could creep in to create division among them. The women had a bond that had developed during the construction of the ark and endured all. But their greatest comfort was praying together and worshipping God for all he had done and for all he was going to do.

> But God remembered Noah and all the wild animals and the livestock that were with him in the ark, and he sent a wind over the earth, and the waters receded. Now the springs of the deep and the floodgates of the heavens had been closed, and the rain had stopped falling from the sky. The

water receded steadily from the earth. At the end of the hundred and fifty days the water had gone down.

Genesis 8:1–3

LAND!

And on the seventeenth day of the seventh month the ark came to rest on the mountains of Ararat. The waters continued to recede until the tenth month, and on the first day of the tenth month the tops of the mountains became visible.

Genesis 8:4–5

Noah and his family got on their knees in preparation to pray before their afternoon meal. They all joined hands in a circle, which had become their preferred method of praying with one another. Noah looked around at the faces of his sons, their wives, and his own wife before he closed his eyes to give thanks and praise.

They had been inside the ark for five months, and they all showed signs of stress, some more than others. Noah prayed for a renewed sense of purpose in their service of the Lord. He prayed today for strength to persevere and for renewed faith for all of them, including himself. He thought of the words he might use for this prayer as he closed his eyes and bowed his head.

Just as he was about to begin, he raised his face toward the heavens above, but before he could speak, there came a loud noise that startled them all. They were not sure where it came from. It seemed to be in the front of the vessel. It was not an animal's call or cry, and it grew louder and seemed to be moving toward them. The others were looking at one another, uncertain whether or not they should panic.

As the sound grew louder, they found that it was difficult to kneel straight, as they felt they were being pushed over. Noah had to let go of his wife's hand to support his unsteady position. Shem and Japheth leaned back in order to maintain their balance, and Ham and his wife had to put their hands down to keep from falling. The strange noise began to sound like something grinding, coming from directly below them. With some difficulty, the men got to their feet and told their wives to wait for them while they went to the lower deck to investigate.

The animals had grown restless, and many of them were pacing around the pens that they had called home for so many months. They were snorting and bleating, mooing and screeching their discontent to the management as the men passed by. The noise the animals were making was loud but not enough to drown out the strange noise from below.

When they reached the bottom deck, they noticed the animals there were exceptionally nervous. They didn't strain against the gates or try to break free, but they clearly objected to whatever was going on. And they made their displeasure known to Noah and his sons. Noah was thankful for those animals that still seemed to be in hibernation. The men walked around slowly, examining the sides and bottom of the ark, but they could see nothing unusual.

The noise here was deafening and still continued beneath their feet, but it had moved beyond them and seemed to be under the whole bottom of the ark. Noah didn't know what it could possibly be. It had to be on the outside, but there was nothing on the outside except water, and of course below the water, the earth.

Noah was leaning slightly over, peering to the sides of the ark and the bottom when he realized what he had just said to himself. He quickly straightened up and his eyes grew wide. Did he dare think such a thing? Shem, who had moved ahead of his father, was on his way back from the front of the ark. He saw his father's face, and it occurred to him as well what the sound could be. He wasn't sure if he should say anything either. His eyes became wide as he moved slowly up to his father.

Ham and Japheth had turned to the back of the ark to examine it, each observing a side of the great vessel. And somewhere on their investigative trek, the same conclusion must have come to them. Whether they figured it out together or one before the other is unclear, but they had no intentions of wondering in awed silence. They came rushing back to their father and brother. As soon as they drew close, they shouted together, "We must have hit something! Ground, we've run aground!"

Noah looked one way slowly and then the other, half expecting to see something or someone. He reached out his arm to Shem, his eyes growing wider, and he turned to reach out to his other sons as they came beside him. He pushed past them, heading for the ramp leading up, never saying a word. As he went beyond them, he pulled on their shoulders as if he had to encourage them to follow him. No coaxing was necessary. They followed directly behind their father as he quickened his pace, heading for the upper deck.

Noah and Shem ran to the nearest window and together pulled it open. Ham and Japheth rushed over to their mother and their wives and announced softly but excitedly the conclusion to which they had come. The women looked at each other, smiled, and embraced one another; it lasted for several moments.

Noah and Shem looked out to see if anything other than water was visible. Obviously the winds had been blowing them along, but there had not really been any sense of moving until something had caused them to stop. Given the size of the ark, it would have to be a big something. The fact that they could see nothing was disappointing, but this did not dampen their excitement for long.

Shem was considering their situation and concluded that the vessel touching ground might not be so unusual. Because of the size and weight of the ark, its bottom very likely sat at least ten to twelve cubits beneath the surface, perhaps even more with the passengers and stores aboard. So if the bottom of the ark had hit ground, it could still be fifteen to eighteen feet below the surface. *But ground is ground!* he thought. And that must mean the waters were receding. Shem explained all this to all of them as they were looking for a sign that God had not forgotten them, and this was what they needed.

Noah had turned from the window and let the shutter close. He was walking very slowly back toward the others. He was speaking to God, thanking him for hearing his prayers before he had even gotten the chance to put them into complete thoughts or words. He was praising the LORD for his might, his mercy, and his attention to all those on the ark. He was praising the God who knew their prayers and thoughts before they were even uttered and answered each of those prayers according to his perfect will. Noah was in awe of God but felt a little embarrassed that he needed to be reminded once again. He asked forgiveness for the doubt that had crept into his mind just a few short moments ago.

As he approached those standing across the floor from him, he reached down for a hand to his right and then a hand to his left. The chatter paused as they wondered if he was about to speak. "Where were we," he began, and he dropped to his knees and closed his eyes. Then he paused, eyes closed, as the others reached for a hand to their right and left and lowered to their knees with Noah. And they prayed.

Noah prayed, and when he stopped, Shem prayed. In fact, each of his sons prayed that afternoon, giving thanks and praise to God for the blessings in their lives. They gave thanks for the sign God had just given them and asked forgiveness for their lack of faith. Ham dwelt longer on his shortcomings in this area, though others confessed their doubts and asked forgiveness as well.

They prayed for strength and endurance in the time to come because they realized that it might still be some time before they would see land, and even longer before they were ready to leave the ark. They gave thanks that the LORD chose them to be here at all. They remembered the last visions before the ark was sealed and the fate of those outside the door. And they worshipped God in all his awesome glory, power, sovereignty, love, mercy, wisdom, and grace.

And as each of the men took turns praising and worshipping God, the others prayed silently from their hearts. And each one of them repented of those things for which they felt ashamed of in going against God's will, doubting God's love and mercy. Every one of them felt as though the LORD had personally touched their shoulder and whispered in their ear that they should not ever again bring up this matter. It was forgiven and forgotten and he would never speak of it again.

That day, and in the days and weeks to come, there was a renewed energy and spirit in the ark. The daily chores and routines that had grown so mundane and were looked upon as unpleasant were no longer seen in that light. Even Ham returned to his true self again, and they went about the routines as they had done when they were first sealed in the ark. The ark seemed to have come to a rest, for the grinding, sliding noises had ceased while they were praying.

Their spirits rose and were renewed even though for many days they strained to see the land as they peered out of the windows, but there was only water and the horizon. They did not let this discourage them, for they knew the waters were receding. After it came to rest on the earth, the big vessel settled more firmly as the waters lowered. It was not drastic, but there was a tilt in the way the ark had settled on the uneven ground.

Noah woke with a start one morning before dawn. He sat upright and paused, wondering if something had wakened him, a noise his subconscious had picked up or a dream he could not recall now that the sleep had left his eyes. He felt as though he had been up for quite some time. He looked around but there was no one else stirring. So Noah decided to rise and spend some quiet time with the LORD.

It had been about seventy-four days since the ark had come to rest on the ground. Things had been so much better after that day they all surrendered their fears and expectations to God. Although there was no sign of land these many days, they did not slip back into the gloomy mood that had threatened their harmony; they remained faithful and waited upon their God. Now it was only every few days that they would look out. Noah figured that sometimes in between those checks his sons likely peeked out now and then, just to be sure.

He got up from his bed quietly and slowly so he would not disturb his wife. Though it was still dark, his eyes adjusted quickly, and he moved to another area so he would have some light without disturbing anyone else. He felt a need to speak with God this morning, as he did every morning. There had been very few times in his adult life that he had not started his day in prayer and worship. And when he failed to do so, it never seemed quite right.

So Noah started this day conversing with God just as he had done so many other days. This day was especially productive. From the time he first knelt in humble submission before God, he felt the presence of God's Spirit with him.

Noah prayed and worshipped a long time that morning. Deep in thought and praise, he felt at times that God was right by his side. Noah felt such incredible joy hearing God speak to him this way. Noah would feel his ears turn red in shame when as they walked God referred to him as his good and faithful servant. Noah knew better than to argue with God, but he wondered if God really had a grasp of whom he was walking with; he felt so unworthy. But he would be reminded that God knew everything, saw everything, and nothing could be hidden from the ever-watchful eyes of the Creator. And in this vision, God would laugh and reassure Noah that he was well aware who he was walking with and speaking to.

It was nothing like Noah had ever felt or dreamed before.

And when he was on his knees again looking around the ark, he wondered if perhaps he had dozed off. But there was energy in his body, awareness in his mind. He felt more awake now than he could ever remember. He remained kneeling, giving thanks for this time he had with God. And when he finally rose, he could see the light from outside peeking around the edges of the windows. Noah thought he might just have a look.

When Japheth rose and came out of his quarters, he looked around to see if anyone else was up. It was daylight outside, and he felt as though he had slept in very late. But it was refreshing. He felt completely rested, as though he had desperately needed the extra sleep.

He was stretching the stiffness out of his limbs when he noticed the windows open ahead of him. The light was stream-ing into the upper deck, and he knew someone else was up. He walked closer and saw his father sitting in the window, looking out. Noah had not heard Japheth come up behind him. Not wanting to startle his father, Japheth called his name softly, and Noah turned to his son. He was smiling, and without a word, he motioned for him to come to the window.

The windows were like large rectangles. They were longer than they were high, about four cubits long and one cubit high. Japheth moved to his father's side, watching his face. It was a strange but reassuring kind of smile. Noah reached gently over to his son staring at him and, putting his hand on the side of his chin, turned his head toward the window. Japheth did not resist, and as his head turned, he began to get the same strange smile his father had. They turned briefly to one another, then back to the open window.

"Father, Japheth?" Shem was standing behind the two men. When they turned to look at Shem, they noticed that the rest of the family was stirring; everyone was up. Shem was looking at them with a puzzled look on his face. "Are you all right? We have been watching you two just sitting here for a while now. You haven't even taken notice of us back here." Noah looked beyond Shem, and there was his wife, Ham, and the other wives moving about, setting up things for a light breakfast and getting ready to start the day.

"No, we had not noticed you back there. Why don't all of you come and join us here? It is a beautiful day outside. Perhaps we should give thanks to God right here." Noah motioned to Japheth with his head. Japheth moved down to the next window and propped it open for the others. Shem called the others and they came to join Noah and Japheth.

Noah and Japheth moved to the next window and left the closer one available to those coming over. Without direction, Noah and Japheth turned back to gaze out of the windows again. Shem looked at the family approaching and shrugged his shoulders. He waited for his wife and the others before they stepped up to look at what Noah and Japheth found so interesting.

There was a collective gasp, and Ham stepped back from the window, his eyes wide and his mouth open. The others grabbed the sill of the window, and their mouths dropped open too; there was a long silence. Ham moved back to the window beside his wife, and they each looked out in awe of the sight before them. Their mouths turned up into a smile; most eyes were filled to overflowing. And they stood there a long while.

Out across the vast ocean of water that had greeted them day after day, week after week, month after month, there were interruptions in the flat line where the water had met the sky on the horizon. Here and there were mountaintops that had risen from the depths since they had last dared to glimpse out. It was amazing. They had seen nothing but water for 224 days straight, and the sight of land was the most beautiful thing they could ever recall.

In the days following, they would open the windows to check on the water levels. With a reference point now, rather than just the horizon where the water met the sky, it was easy to see the water receding daily. More and more of the mountaintops came into sight. There was no way to determine the height of these mountains, so there was no way to tell how far the waters had to recede before the earth would be dry enough to leave the ark.

Forty days had passed since the mountaintops had been exposed by the receding waters. Then, on the tenth day of the eleventh month, Noah felt a calling from the LORD. He slowly reached up to the corner where the rafter and beam met at the wall of the ark. This had been a favorite roost for the ravens for a long time. And more times than not this was the place they chose to spend the evenings. It was too dark to tell if the bird was awake or not, but it did not seem to notice him reaching up. Either that or the LORD was calming the bird so it would not fly away.

Standing on a bench he had pulled over so he could reach the bird, Noah still had to rise up on his tiptoes. He wanted to catch the bird, but he wanted to be as gentle with it as possible. He was concerned that if it tried to struggle and he did not have a good grasp on it, it might injure itself trying to escape. So Noah had set in his mind that at any sign of flapping or alarm on the part of the bird, if it were not firmly in his full grasp, he would just let it go and either try something different or look for another subject.

When he put his hands directly over and around the raven that was standing perfectly still, he knew he could reach far enough to get a good firm but gentle grip. But suddenly the bird cawed loudly and turned to face the man sneaking up behind him. Immediately Noah withdrew his hands to his sides. He looked at the raven, and the raven, now facing him, looked right back at him. He expected the bird to either fly away or move to another location higher and out of reach. But it just stood there watching him. It cocked its head sideways as though it were studying the man before him. Then it began to flap its wings, but it did not fly away. It seemed to be stretching them, as though it had just awakened.

Noah's sons were just behind him, watching with much anticipation. From the start they had been observing with such concentration that it appeared as if their movements and Noah's were one in the same. Now they settled back into a stealth mode as Noah began to slowly reach up toward the bird once again.

Noah knew the bird was definitely awake and watching his

every move. He thought if he could keep the bird focused on his face and eyes, it might not notice his hands slowly but surely maneuvering into position. But the bird was more interested in those hands coming towards him than in the man's face. The face was well out of the bird's comfort zone, but these two things moving towards him from each side were something different. Noah could see he was not fooling this small creature in the least, but he did not give up. He was concerned that the bird would fly before he got close enough to clasp him in his hands, but to his pleasant surprise, he was wrong.

Japheth, Ham, and Shem were twisting their faces into expressions of intense concentration and grim determination as they followed Noah's actions to catch the bird as he reached toward it from his position below. They did not notice the women giggling at the spectacle as they watched from the distance. This was the best entertainment they had in a very long time.

Noah continued moving his hands towards the raven, slowly up and over the beam until they were within inches of the bird's body. The raven was obviously very nervous and very aware of the hands closing in on him. He rocked back and forth but did not try to escape. Noah realized at this point that the bird was not attempting to flee from him. So rather than making a quick grab, Noah eased his hands around its body and lifted it off of its perch. His sons below had been holding their breath as his hands got closer and closer, and then all three let out a collective sigh as their father picked up the raven.

Noah turned around on the bench to face his sons and the women. He looked puzzled for a moment as he saw his sons' faces. Each of them were flushed and appeared as if they were out of breath. What had they been up to while he was catching the raven? He looked at them a moment wondering but then turned proudly to the women. His wife was raising her eyebrows and nodding in approval. She playfully poked the other women with her elbow as if to say, "Did you see what my husband just did?" Noah grinned, feeling very pleased with himself. He quietly thanked God for helping him. He didn't realize he had such an audience.

Shem went over to his father and reached a hand up to help him get down from the bench. The bird was struggling, but not very much. It was new and unusual for him to be in the grasp of a human, but he was tolerating it as best he could. He could sense that there was no harm meant at all.

Noah walked over to the windows, and Ham rushed ahead of him to prop open the closest one. Japheth and Shem followed behind Noah as he slowly walked to the opening. Noah tried to be very conscious of the pressure he was putting on the bird, wanting to maintain control but not hurt the raven in the process.

As he reached the window, he switched the bird to his left hand. Once Noah had firm grip on it, he put his right hand under the bird's feet hanging beneath his hand. He extended his index finger under the bird's feet, and it reflexively grabbed hold of the finger with its toes. The family stood back together and watched anxiously.

Slowly, Noah released his grip on the raven, and the bird stood on his finger. It shook itself briskly trying to straighten any ruffled feathers. It looked back at Noah and cawed loudly. This was either a thanks for release or an admonishment for being too rough. Maybe it was a little bit of both. Then it turned its head toward the outside. Noah extended his arm until the bird was through the window. The breeze blew the bird's feathers as it closed its eyes briefly.

Then opening them again, the raven bent its legs for momentum, stretched its wings, and flew off the hand of Noah. Everyone quickly gathered around the windows, watching the bird fly high into the sky and disappear. It had been forty days since the ark had come to rest on solid ground.

> After forty days Noah opened the window he had made in the ark and sent out a raven, and it kept flying back and forth until the water had dried up from the earth.
>
> Genesis 8:6–7

The sun climbed high into the sky as Noah stood near the window looking out beyond the opening of the window. He breathed a heavy sigh and closed his eyes for a moment. "I don't think it's coming back."

Noah felt the hand of his wife on his shoulder, and he turned to face her. He had prayed for some sign from God through the bird that would tell him how things were progressing on the earth. But he had realized too that the raven was not going to return. He reached his hand out to her and pulled her close to him. They looked out the window together for a little while. Then Noah spoke, "I know the raven will not return. I was just so certain that God would bring us a sign through the bird. The ravens were always close by, and when I had the dream about a bird with a sign … " He looked into her eyes and she looked into his. He did not finish the sentence.

They turned back to the window as they heard a noise. It was like a whistling, and then there was the sound of a flutter behind them. They turned to see another bird flying up from the second deck over toward the window where they stood. Noah felt her movement before he heard the noise, and he turned in the same direction. A dove was flying down, its wings wide and cupped to slow its descent as it landed on the windowsill. Noah looked at it for a moment and smiled to himself. He would always be in awe of God's creation, whether he was studying the simple complexity of a leaf or one of his winged creatures. Signs of God were all around in everything he saw. But Noah was too distracted by the raven's disappearance to focus for very long.

"Why not try a different bird?" Noah's wife offered the option. She watched the dove walking back and forth on the sill cooing and bobbing its head. Noah looked over to her with some response forming in his mind, but it never developed into a complete thought. He saw that she was not looking at him but at the dove on the window. He had been so caught up in the fact that the raven was gone he never paid attention to this dove that had come right to him.

His eyes diverted from his wife over to the bird as it walked back and forth. This time, as it came toward Noah, it continued until it had actually walked up on to his hand and stopped there. He looked at the dove on his hand then back to her. She shrugged her shoulders and smiled. Then as she turned away, she offered her explanation, "Maybe God?"

Noah felt very blessed as he realized he had been so caught up in the failure of his plan that he almost missed God's plan right there in front of him! His eyes darted upwards and he felt a little embarrassed. He raised his hand with the dove on it, and it remained there, clinging to his finger as the raven had. He put his hand out of the window and closed his eyes to pray for God to give him a sign. As he prayed, he felt the dove lift off his hand and heard the whistling of its wings on the wind as it flew away. He opened his eyes and watched the bird disappear.

Throughout the remainder of the day, Noah passed by the window and paused to stare out into the sky, thinking he just might see one of the birds returning. And then he would return to his task at hand. Everyone on the ark was just as preoccupied about the birds' possible return. If they did not, it could be a sign. If they did return, that too would be an indication, but one with a different outcome. But time after time, they would see Noah turn away from the window with nothing new to share.

Late that same afternoon, as the sun began to sink low, Noah turned away once more, trying not to look disappointed. He was walking back toward the ramp leading to the second level just as his wife was approaching. As he saw her coming toward him, he was determined to put on his best face, not wanting her to see any disappointment in his eyes. He straightened up and put on a smile and thought of how much he loved this woman walking toward him.

She saw her husband coming toward her, but she could not see the expression on his face because of the dazzling glare from the open window behind him. All she could make out was his silhouette from his chest upwards. As Noah drew near to her, he saw her eyes suddenly widen as a surprised and startled look came over her face. And then he heard the whistling in the air behind him.

He turned quickly to see a brilliant light coming through the window and right in the center of that, as if in slow motion, the silhouette of a bird landing, its wings open wide, flapping to slow and steady itself as it landed on the sill of the open window. Now Noah's eyes grew wide and he rushed back to the window. It was the dove he had sent out early in the afternoon. She was slowly strutting back and forth on the sill.

It was not easy for human eyes to see the exhaustion in the bird, but she was just that, exhausted. She had found no place to rest and had been flying around since she had left the ark. Noah reached out and brought her back into the ark. He held her close to his chest as he carried her to a post inside, stroking her gently until he put her down. He was grateful she had made it back, but there was no sign yet from the Lord. And Noah knew he must wait before sending her out again.

At the end of seven days, the family gathered at the window. Shem was opening the cover just as Noah was walking slowly toward the opening with the dove on his hand. It was not necessary to chase or sneak up on her because she had come right to Noah and landed on his hand when he extended his arm. It was early morning and yet the light was full. Everyone stood back just a little, not wanting to startle the dove.

When he got to the window, Noah looked over at Shem standing to his right side. He smiled a well-here-we-go sort of smile as he said a silent prayer. Earlier, before going to get the dove, the family had prayed together. And as Noah prayed aloud for a sign from God this day, each of the others included their personal prayer to the Father about sending the dove out. "Thank you, Lord, for all the blessings you have given each one of us." He opened his eyes again. And with a single fluid motion, he swept his arm forward and extended his hand as the dove took to the air. She had not needed any coaxing to stretch her wings, and immediately she turned to the right, flew away, and quickly disappeared from view.

When Noah could no longer see her or hear her wings on the morning air, he turned around. The look on everyone's faces was one of hope and anxious anticipation.

From where they sat up on the mountaintop, they could not see the land below or distinguish if the waters had receded completely. They knew the waters were going down, but how much further and how much longer before they could once again venture out into the earth was God's unknown plan; he had not revealed it to Noah yet. So they were very anxious about the dove's mission.

It was not completely clear to them how they would know or what sign they might receive, but they sensed God would send them something in his perfect time. And just as he had patiently waited 120 years before bringing the waters on the earth, his timing would be perfect in receding the waters as well. They completely understood how their timing, or the way they thought things should be, was not always in conjunction with God's timing. But if they waited on him, they knew they could not go wrong.

They prayed daily for God to help them increase their faith and remain focused on his plan. And God increased their faith daily. As they gathered to pray this day, Noah went to his wife and held her close, leaning over to gently kiss her forehead. Shem went to his wife as Japheth and Ham sat close to their wives. For a few moments they just held one another. Again, each one praised God silently for all he had delivered them from.

The chores and duties for their days were the same as they had been since they came into the ark nine months earlier. Each one went about the tasks they needed to accomplish with everyone contributing. Every now and then, Noah would stop by the window to see if he could spot the dove returning, but he did not despair; he felt certain she would come back in God's time.

At the midday meal, everyone gathered and ate silently after prayer. They did not sit around after the meal but moved on to continue their tasks. As Noah went about setting out fresh water for the animals, he began to think of what would come next. He knew that eventually the Lord would have them leave the ark and go out into the world. But there was nothing in the world any longer. The population of the earth was contained within the walls of the ark, with the exception of a dove and perhaps a raven.

Noah prayed that the new earth would be so much better than the last. He prayed that his sons and their wives and the children they would bring into the world would all be brought up to praise, honor, and totally rely on God. He prayed that they would never turn away from God's love. It was an awesome opportunity, and he prayed that God had chosen the right man in him. Doubt crept into his mind, not because of God but because of his human nature. He wondered if he had done all he could as he raised his sons to follow God and to serve him.

The sun was sinking low toward the horizon, and evening would be upon them soon. As Noah was coming up the ramp to the third level, he thought of lowering the shutter for the evening, and so he started toward the open window. He decided to look around just one more time while the light allowed.

He placed his hands on the open sill and was about to poke his head out for a better view when the whistling of wings seemed to come out of nowhere and the dove landed on the sill as if she had just appeared. He had been so focused on his own thoughts he had not heard her coming in for a landing. It startled him for a moment, and once again he was glad she had made it back to the safety of the ark.

The others had heard the familiar whistling of her wings and the coos she made as she strutted up and down the surface of the sill. They all came running to Noah. And just as they were arriving, Noah realized that she was carrying something in her beak. He gently reached for the object, and she released her grip on it as soon as his fingers grasped it. He drew it slowly to himself, and his eyes grew wide when he realized what he was holding. As he turned to the family, the dove flew inside the ark, seeking her mate to settle in for a good rest.

Noah held out the little green olive leaf as he walked forward, a smile growing wider with each step. It was a sign of new growth in the earth. This was the sign they had hoped for. Life had begun again on the face of the earth.

Shem, Ham, and Japheth gathered together with their father

to discuss what the olive leaf meant to them and their immediate future. Of course, they were anxious to open the ark and feel the earth beneath their feet once again.

It had been two days since the dove returned, and it did not seem as though Noah was in any hurry to leave the ark. His sons explained how they viewed things and presented their case to their father. First, Noah noticed that each of his sons had different ideas on certain details. He thought that was a good thing, and he listened patiently to all they had to say. When they had finished and they had nothing further to add, they stared at their father. He just sat there saying nothing.

"Well?" Ham asked.

"Well, what?" Noah responded. "I didn't hear a question posed to me. I've just been listening to your plans once we exit the ark." He paused and then asked, "Is there a question?"

Ham seemed a little exasperated. "Yes, there is a question! When are we leaving the ark? That is what all this discussion has been about; when are we going out?"

Noah looked at them for a long moment and then rose to his feet. "Sons, we have been spared from the destruction of the earth by God. All of my life I have relied on God to guide me. Since he first spoke to me and told me that I should build this ark and why, he has been guiding us each step of this amazing journey. You were not even born when he told me to build this ark to save my wife, sons, and their wives. The ark came together piece by piece only by the power and grace of our Lord. We all saw the animals gather, and not one entered the ark until the Lord spoke telling us it was time."

Noah looked at his sons and paused for a long time before continuing. "God will tell us when it is time to leave the ark. God has not spoken to me, so we will remain here until I hear from him. And that is all the answer we need; God will provide. It is not for us to completely understand the will of our Creator. But let's think about this from our own perspective."

He sat down again and looked up into each face. There was some disappointment in the eyes of each of his sons. But there was an acceptance and understanding there also. Noah continued, "We know the earth and the seasons, and we know the growth cycles of the trees and plants. We have seen a new olive leaf. Does the tree that the leaf came from have olives? No, they have not come out. If all things are beginning again, they are just starting their cycle of life. If we leave the ark carrying what provisions we can and go down the mountain, how long will it be before we can harvest food? If we harvest too soon, if the animals we release eat the tender shoots and grasses before they flower and bear fruit, what have we accomplished? God is healing the earth, preparing a place for us. Of course we are anxious to begin a new life again, but we must be patient. We must have faith that when it is time, God will tell us. We shall not go before God's time." He looked at them as he finished what he had to say.

Then he walked past the three standing together, pondering their father's words. Noah put his hand on each shoulder as he walked past and returned to the upper decks.

> He waited seven more days and sent the dove out again, but this time it did not return to him.

> Genesis 8:12

Noah and his family had been in the ark now for 314 days. It had been over a month since Noah had released the dove again, and she had not returned to the ark. Though his sons and the women had tried to be patient and wait for the right time to go out, it was obvious that everyone was restless and wanted to be off the ark. From their windows high up near the roof of the ark, there was a very limited view of the surrounding areas. All they could see were some surrounding mountaintops and the sky when they looked out.

It was a special day for the passengers of the ark; they were preparing for a better view of the earth around them. Noah, Shem, Ham, and Japheth were positioned at the sides of the ark near the roof. They were preparing to remove the large wooden pegs that had been driven into place to secure the roof panels when the ark had been built. At first it seemed as though the pegs would not budge as the men had positioned themselves on each corner of the panel. Then Noah's peg began to move. After so long a time, they were not easily broken loose. Once it started to shift though, it went easier.

When he had gotten the peg at this corner out, he moved over to Japheth, who was still pounding at the peg in his position. Soon it gave way, as did the ones Shem and Ham had been working on. Once all of the pegs had been removed, the men again positioned themselves under the first panel and tried to work it up and out of the saddle it had rested in for all this time.

There was lots of grunting and straining before each side began to lift out of its place. Carefully they slid this first panel out over the top of the ark. As the panel slid behind them, Noah turned to see what he could see. He actually climbed out on to the top of the ark. The sight nearly took his breath away. His sons, who had been sliding the panel completely out of the way, had paused once it was done and were watching their father's reaction as he stood outside and looked around. They had seen his mouth drop open as he slowly and without a word started walking to the edge of the vessel.

Unable to wait any longer, the sons clambered out, one after another, to see the view for themselves. There was a cool, refreshing breeze blowing from the north as the four men stood side by side, atop the ark, which was atop the mountain the vessel had settled on. All around them, they could see the dry land. There were grasses, trees, meadows, and streams below. Everything was more lush and green than they had ever remembered it being. Trees were flowering, though from their position it was impossible to tell what type of trees or distinguish the flowers. They could see the green canopies speckled with multitudes of colors. The colors and shapes and terrain all blended together, but as far as the eye could see, the earth was green and dry.

For a long time they stood watching everything around them, peering off in all directions, taking in the magnificent vistas. But Noah finally called them back inside the ark to continue working at removing the panels that made up the covering of the ark. Not long after, Noah and Shem set up some steps where the women could come out of the ark and take in the beauty as well. The look on each of their faces as they gazed out over all that God had created was one of awe, of thanks and praise, and one of worship.

Noah's wife never said a word, but simply brought her hands to her breast and stared as though she needed to be sure she could feel her heartbeat and know she was still breathing. It was the most beautiful sight she had ever seen.

THE NEW COVENANT

By the twenty-seventh day of the second month the earth was completely dry. Then God said to Noah, "Come out of the ark, you and your wife and your sons and their wives. Bring out every kind of living creature that is with you—the birds, the animals, and all the creatures that move along the ground—so they can multiply on the earth and be fruitful and increase in number upon it."

Genesis 8:14–17

When Noah and his family had been inside the ark for 370 days, God again called on Noah. Noah was putting more hay over and into the section where the young doe and buck were kept. Their new baby, a small spotted fawn, was positioning itself under the hay as Noah reached over the fencing. It was obviously going to try to get an advance sampling before the other animals had the chance to move in.

"Noah!" Noah was taken aback. He had not expected to hear the voice of God at that moment, and it startled him. He felt a little embarrassed, especially since he dropped the armload of hay directly atop the fawn. It did not hurt the little one, only startled it slightly and perhaps dented its dignity a bit. It was trying to shake the pieces of straw from its head, nose, and ears. The fawn was not sure what had happened, but it was obvious the little baby did not care for the experience at all.

"Come out of the ark, you and your wife and your sons and their wives." Noah's eyes grew wide as the instructions were given and the message sank in. This was the call they had been praying and waiting so long for! Noah drew in a quick breath as the words of the LORD came over him and what they would mean to him and his family. "Bring out every kind of living creature that is with you—the birds, the animals, and all the creatures that move along the ground—so they can multiply on the earth and be fruitful and increase in number upon it."

Noah felt God's presence long after the words had been spoken; he stood there silently praising and worshipping his holy name. The LORD had given them so much and had provided for them through all of this without asking or expecting anything in return. And now Noah and his family were to go out with all the creatures that move on the land, fly through the air, and creep on the earth and start a new world. It was in that moment that Noah realized what he must do.

He walked from where he stood on the middle deck to where the doorway of the ark was. From the deck above, Shem was walking by and happened to glance down to where his father was slowly and methodically approaching the door. He had no idea that anything out of the ordinary was going on, but for some reason he paused to watch.

Just a moment later, Japheth looked up from where he was tending some animals. With no real reason or purpose, he rose and moved over to the side of his brother Shem. When he reached his side, he instinctively looked from Shem down to his father, who was just now reaching the large doorway the LORD had sealed behind them over a year ago when the waters came and filled the earth.

Noah stood there for a moment, and then hesitantly he pushed against the doorway. It did not move. From above through the dim light, neither Shem nor Japheth could really tell what he had done. Noah's eyes wandered slowly from the bottom on the left side of the door, up to the top, across the top, and then down the right side to the bottom of the door as though he were searching for something. Then he turned back to the center, put his hands up to the doorway again, and pushed, a little more forcefully this time, but nothing happened.

The movement was a little more pronounced to the two men above, and then Shem realized what his father was attempting to do. He looked at Japheth as he started moving down the adjoining ramp between the decks toward his father. "Call the others!" he told Japheth and hurried down to his father. Japheth read the excitement in Shem's eyes before he turned to go down. Then he too realized what was happening and began calling the others to come quickly.

Shem reached his father's side in no time and stood beside him facing the door. Noah, who had been studying the door in deep concentration, looked over at his son and without a word turned back to the door once more. He and Shem both put their arms to the door and pushed. This time they both put their shoulders behind the effort.

Just as the family was gathering around them, there was a loud creaking noise and a jerking movement at the top of the door. As Noah and Shem stepped back, a crack of light appeared at the top of the opening, and in a smooth, almost fluid motion, the light poured in as the doorway lowered into an open position. It stopped the descent at a slight angle downward from the level of the deck as it came to rest on a small knoll or ridge just beside where the LORD had brought the ark to rest. Now full light and the cool morning breeze came flooding into the lower decks that had been only dimly lit at best for the past year. As the door lowered down, Ham and the women were frozen in their tracks.

The animals became excited, and the typically quiet, serene ark was filled with calls, grunts, bleats, howls, and whistles as each of the animals praised the LORD in their own way. Noah stood at the opening, gazing out of the ark and down the gradual slope of the mountainside where they had landed. The remainder of the family joined him and Shem there as each one stared out at the beauty of the land. They were silently pouring their hearts out with thanks and praise to the awesome God that had blessed them all with a grace and mercy that they never could have possibly dreamed of. They were ready to go out and feel the grass beneath their feet and leave this vessel of salvation provided by God. But, as though it were an unspoken command, none moved before Noah did, and he just stood there. When he finally did speak, it was as if he had read their minds.

"'Bring out with you every living thing of all flesh that is with you,' is what God told me," he related to the others. "Before we go out, we must take care of the creatures God has entrusted to our care." With that said, he turned to go back in.

Shem and Japheth turned immediately and followed after their father. Ham hesitated a short while, soaking up a little more of the sense of freedom before he turned to go back into the ark. Then Noah's wife turned and went up to the upper decks to gather their belongings. As she worked, she wondered where they would go, where they would settle and rebuild a home. She looked forward to having another place she could call home. Her sons' wives worked with her, and at her direction, they began sorting things out for each of their households. They began to realize that they would be starting their own households now; they would begin a new life with their husbands and families.

The men began opening the pens, taking down gates and barriers, and releasing the animals. At first the creatures just stayed where they were; they had become accustomed to the surroundings and the people they saw each day for so long. It did not cross their minds that they should go out, multiply, and fill the earth.

Noah walked over to the doe and buck he had been feeding earlier when God spoke. He moved to the doe's side, stroked her neck, and spoke softly to her, coaxing her to follow him. She had no clue what he was saying, but the calm stroke and mellow voice seemed to beckon her. So when Noah started walking out of the pen toward the door, she followed, along with the buck and their new baby, who stayed very close.

As though it were a signal to every creature in the ark, the animals all began to move. From below, Japheth and Shem urged the creatures that began to follow towards the ramp. Ham came down from the upper deck, and behind him, the creatures followed. They merged in the middle, and just as their entrance to the ark had been calm and organized, the departure was the same. Noah and his family came out first and moved to the ridge at the bottom of the doorway and stood aside watching the exodus.

Some animals wandered to the side of the path that had been formed and began to graze, tasting the new grass. But most kept moving forward on down the side of the mountain. The birds came out, and while most just took flight, some of the larger ones walked until they cleared the doorway and then spread their huge wings; they took flight to a new destination.

Just as they had been brought to Noah, it appeared the animals were being directed by God to their new homes, new lands. The creatures looked around at their surroundings as they came out, but they seemed to know just exactly which direction they were to go as they started down the mountain. It was an amazing sight to see.

In just a short time, a line of creatures of every type and size was heading off towards the plains below as far as the humans could see. Most moved in pairs, but in many cases by families, as some such as the ducks, deer, and bears had babies during the time they were inside the ark. Noah and his family could not know that others such as the elephant or the behemoth were both expecting babies to be born within a year or more after they had left the mountain.

Throughout the day the animals filed out of the ark. Some creatures, such as the snails that needed a head start, received assistance from the humans. Many of them became excited and frisky once they reached the open areas. No doubt, there had been a lot of pent up energy waiting for so long to be released.

The horses took off at a full gallop as soon as they reached the bottom of the ramp. They never stopped or slowed until they were out of sight of the ark. Their manes and tails were flowing like sails, their hooves thundering on the slopes, then fading as the distance between them and the ark grew. The gazelles were leaping high into the air in a wide sweeping arc as they ran down the mountain towards the open plain.

Noah watched the parade for some time before he moved away from the doorway and out onto the land. He chose a level spot that rose above the ridge just a short distance away. Without a word to anyone, he began gathering stones and piling them together. It was Shem that first noticed he was no longer with them, and he wandered away from the others to see where his father had gone. He walked along the ridge toward the back of the ark. And before he had gotten to the back of the vessel, he noticed Noah off to his right on an elevated position, carrying a large stone. He wandered over to the site and saw him put the stone on an organized pile that had been started then turn away to seek another.

When Shem came near, Noah was returning with yet another stone. He strained under the weight of it, but he had a determined look in his eyes. Noah turned to Shem as he walked up to the other stones. "Care to lend a hand?" Noah asked as he put the stone carefully into place. He straightened up and stretched backwards, putting his hands at his waist, attempting to release the tension in his back.

"Exactly what are we doing?" asked Shem, following his father as he went off to find another stone.

"We are building an altar."

Shem was not familiar with the altars to which Noah referred because it was not often that they had seen one. In fact, all of Noah's sons had been too young to remember the last altar they had seen nearly one hundred years ago. But Shem sought out stones similar to those his father had found.

And when Noah had built an altar, he gathered his family

and gathered the animals he would sacrifice as burnt offerings to the LORD. As he offered the burnt offerings, Noah prayed aloud, "Father, God of creation, ruler of all things seen and unseen, Deliverer, God of redemption, we stand before you to offer our praise and our worship to you. LORD, you give and you take away according to your plan. Father, we know that nothing happens apart from your perfect will. We cannot explain it, but you have chosen us, Almighty LORD, to survive the flood that you brought upon the wickedness and sin that had consumed the earth. Father, we know we are not worthy of such an honor, but in your grace and mercy, my family was chosen. May we never forget this blessing, and we thank you, oh God, for the direction and guidance each day during the time the ark was being built. We know the skills and strength to complete this mighty task were not from our own capabilities but were divinely provided to my family and myself.

"We ask your forgiveness for our impatience, for our lack of faith in your complete deliverance during the time in the ark. You have never failed us before, oh LORD, yet we doubted during that time. All we needed to do was think back on all you have done in our lives, and we may not have stumbled. But we are human; we are sinful by nature, and we think in terms of our abilities and our endurance and our understanding. But LORD, God, Creator, and Deliverer, your ways are so far above ours that we can never see things as you do.

"We pray that each day we may know more according to your will, but we understand that it is not for man to know all of your ways. So we ask you to strengthen our faith so we may not stumble as often as we are prone." Noah's hands were held open and high in the air as he prayed. Behind him, his wife, their sons, and their wives were all on their knees, some with raised arms and faces, some with bowed heads and clenched palms.

"LORD God, Father of all creation," Noah continued, "we make this small offering to you, not as a payment for the things you have done for us, because there is nothing we have or could ever obtain that would be worthy to offer for what you do for us, but as a symbol of our thanks, our praise, and our worship. We pray you find this offering pleasing and accept it as our way of showing how much we desire to know and follow you all of our days.

"LORD, my words are simply your humble servant's expression to you. I know they are not sufficient, as this burnt offering is not sufficient. But I know that you can see our hearts and know our minds. I pray that my heart will never cause you to hurt, dear Father. I pray that no one in this family nor the generations to come will ever stray far from your protection, your grace, and your mercy."

Noah then dropped to his knees. He had so much more to be thankful for, but he knew there was nothing more he could say that God did not already know. He bowed his head, and the entire family stayed that way as the offering burned before them.

> The LORD smelled the pleasing aroma and said in his heart: "Never again will I curse the ground because of man, even though every inclination of his heart is evil from childhood. And never again will I destroy all living creatures, as I have done. As long as the earth endures, seedtime and harvest, cold and heat, summer and winter, day and night will never cease.

> Genesis 8:21–22

Shem, Ham, and Japheth were kneeling directly behind Noah before the altar. All of them were deep in prayer, giving thanks, asking forgiveness, guidance, and wisdom from the one true God. As they knelt there, they literally felt the breath of God come over them. This was not a breeze such as they had felt earlier, but something totally different. None of them had any doubt that it was from above. The feeling that came over them caused the hair on their arms to stand on end, and they felt a chill run up and down their bodies. Not a chill from the cold, but a sensation that traveled from head to foot through their body bringing a sensation of peace, overwhelming thankfulness, and joy to their hearts.

And God blessed Noah and his sons and said to them, "Be fruitful and multiply, and fill the earth." This was the first time Shem, Ham, and Japheth had actually heard God speak, and he was speaking to them! Noah clenched his eyes tight and bowed his head, unable to contain the tears. He was at a loss to understand how his Lord could speak to him again. He would never get used to the idea that the Creator of all things spoke to him.

Shem, Ham, and Japheth were totally overwhelmed as well. Shem fell forward to his face with his arms stretched out before him, his entire body tense, excited and humbled all at the same time. Japheth fell backwards, his eyes wide with awe, and he too was finding it difficult to believe he was hearing God's voice. He looked at his brothers and father, and he grasped at the reality of this experience; it was not a figment of his imagination! He clumsily tried to get back to his knees, begging forgiveness from God for his awkwardness.

Ham just slumped from the kneeling position to a sitting position on the back of his calves and heels. He could not contain the tears as a wave of emotion came over him also. He bowed his head and clenched his hands tightly together as God continued to speak: "The fear of you and the terror of you will be on every beast of the earth and on every bird of the sky; with everything that creeps on the ground, and all the fish of the sea, into your hand they are given. Every moving thing that is alive shall be food for you; I give all to you, as I gave the green plant. Only you shall not eat flesh with its life, that is, its blood. Surely I will require your lifeblood; from every beast I will require it."

Despite the awe, the reverent fear, and the amazement of all they were experiencing, Noah and his sons took in every word as the Lord put it in their minds and their hearts to carry throughout their lives. The women had backed away a little, huddled together and shuddering, their eyes closed and tears streaming without end as they listened to God address the men. None of them had ever doubted that Noah had truly spoken to

God before, but nothing had prepared them to actually hear the Almighty LORD of all speaking in their presence.

"And from each man, too, I will demand an accounting for the life of his fellow man. Whoever sheds the blood of man, by man shall his blood be shed; for in the image of God has God made man."

At this point, Noah opened his eyes and relaxed a little. He slumped down momentarily and then slowly rose to his feet. He looked around as though he had just come out of a trance, and he saw his sons still frozen in the positions they had taken when God began to speak; their eyes were tightly closed. The rise and fall of their chest cavities was the only sign to distinguish them from statues. The women, he noticed, were in a tight circle, holding hands, all on their knees with their heads bowed. He could see their lips moving, almost in unison with one another, but there was no sound emitting from their lips as their silent prayers went up to the LORD.

Noah moved over to Shem who was closest to him and put his hand on his shoulder as he stooped to reach his son's prostrate body. At first there was a jump when Noah touched him, but in an instant, Shem realized this was not the hand of God. He raised his head slowly and saw his father beside him. His eyes were red, as were his father's; they both had an understanding smile on their faces. Noah stood and moved over to Ham as Shem brought himself upright and tried to rise. He felt exhilarated, but there seemed to be no strength in his limbs as he attempted to stand.

Noah reached down to Ham and touched his shoulder. Slowly his eyes opened, and he looked up at his father. There was a twinge of disappointment in his eyes when he realized it was not God, but it did absolutely nothing to take away from the experience none of them would ever forget. Noah looked deep into his son's eyes, and Ham saw a light he had not noticed before. He knew it was a small remnant of the Spirit of God from inside his father. He wondered, mainly because he felt it within himself, if he had a similar light in his own eyes.

Noah reached his hand down to Ham, offering to help him

to his feet. Ham accepted and found it a chore to simply raise his arm. He had never poured out his heart and soul to God like this before. And though his body was drained of strength, his heart and his mind had never been so alive. He wanted to praise God each day as he had this afternoon on top of the mountains of Ararat.

No word was spoken by any as Noah moved on to Japheth, who was laughing and reached to his father for a hand up. His eyes too were red and wet, but his heart was dancing with joy. He wanted to rise quickly and hug his father, but he needed help. Noah reached down and offered his hand to Japheth. As he rose to his feet, Japheth could not help but wonder, had his father felt this each time the LORD spoke to him? He wanted to ask, he wanted to shout with joy and praise, but no words would come. So he continued laughing. Noah was smiling with a total understanding as he helped Japheth to his feet, and the two embraced.

Shem and Ham were still trying to get used to their legs again as they were following Noah, who now turned his attention to the women. As Noah reached the circle of women, he reached down and put his hands on his wife's shoulders. He did not raise her up but knelt down beside her. As she broke the hold with the other women, she pulled Noah close to her and held him tight. He smiled knowingly as her hold was stronger than he had ever felt in all their years of marriage. She had always been, next to the LORD, the most important thing in his life, and he in hers. But the bond they felt now was closer, more secure, and more comforting than they had ever experienced.

As she held him, she tried to understand how he must have felt those times that God had called to him. The women had been blessed to witness the exchange, and she felt as though her life would never be the same because of it. As Noah and his wife were holding one another, Shem, Ham, and Japheth moved to their wives and they all embraced, sharing the exhilaration, the joy, and the wonder of the moment.

Then God spoke to Noah and to his sons with him, saying, "I now establish my covenant with you and with your descendants after you and with every living creature that was with you—the birds, the livestock and all the wild animals, all those that came out of the ark with you—every living creature on earth. I establish my covenant with you: Never again will all life be cut off by the waters of a flood; never again will there be a flood to destroy the earth."

When God began speaking to Noah and his sons again, they immediately rose. The weakness in their limbs had disappeared, and they stood together, slowly moving towards the altar. Though the voice seemed to be all around them and in them, the men stood side by side with their faces turned towards heaven and their eyes closed tightly. The words came to them, and they not only heard the promise, they received it. And the words the LORD spoke to each of them were burned in their hearts, their minds, and their souls.

God said, "This is the sign of the covenant I am making between me and you and every living creature with you, a covenant for all generations to come: I have set my rainbow in the clouds, and it will be the sign of the covenant between me and the earth. Whenever I bring clouds over the earth and the rainbow appears in the clouds, I will remember my covenant between me and you and all living creatures of every kind. Never again will the waters become a flood to destroy all life. Whenever the rainbow appears in the clouds, I will see it and remember the everlasting covenant between God and all living creatures of every kind on the earth."

When the LORD finished speaking these words, they opened their eyes. The women rose and moved to the side of the men, each woman next to her husband. They could see the men looking into the sky over the ark, and their eyes grew wide as they witnessed what the men were staring at. God's covenant, just as he had spoken of, was in the clouds before them. The arc of colors was vivid, and they extended beyond the length of the vessel, front and back. It was the first rainbow, and there has not been another like it since that day. The red, orange, yellow, green, blue, indigo, and violet hues seemed to be lit by an unknown source of light. Rather than looking like a refraction of light off tiny particles of water in the air, this one seemed to be three-dimensional!

> So God said to Noah, "This is the sign of the covenant I have established between me and all life on the earth."

Genesis 9:17

Then all of them gathered what they could carry and drove their small herds down to the valley below. They knew they needed to get down from the mountain, and so they did not wait to get started. There was very little said on the way down. Each person that had witnessed the events of the day was processing all they had seen and heard and felt. They did not notice that the animals already had disappeared into their new habitats. Those that were selected to stay in this area did not show themselves to the humans that had cared for them in the past year. Terror of the people had already come on every beast of the earth and on every bird of the sky and everything that creeps on the ground and all the fish of the sea, just as the LORD had spoken. When they had nearly reached the plains below, the sun was sinking low.

Shem turned to get a last glimpse of the ark, though he was not certain he would be able to see it from the path they were on. When he stopped, he turned and called to his father. Noah turned and came back to his son. The others stopped also, and when Noah reached Shem, his son pointed back up the mountain in the direction they had come. The rainbow was still as bright and vivid as ever; dark gray clouds all around the mountaintop made it seem to stand out even more.

But it was not the sign of God's promise that caught Shem's attention. It was the tiny white flecks that rained down on the mountaintop, already creating a white mantle over the area they had left. And even to this day, the mountains of Ararat have snowcaps that do not melt, but snow and ice are built up day after day, concealing the evidence of God's plan for salvation in the time of Noah until he is ready to reveal it to all.

Noah watched the snow fall for a few moments and then turned, reaching out for Shem's shoulder as he did. Then the two joined the rest of the family, continuing their journey into the valley and out into the earth.

> The sons of Noah who came out of the ark were Shem, Ham and Japheth. (Ham was the father of Canaan.) These were the three sons of Noah, and from them came the people who were scattered over the earth.
>
> Genesis 9:18–19